Dorothy B. Hughes and The Murder Room

》》》 This title is part of The Murder Room, our series dedicated to making available out-of-print or hard-to-find titles by classic crime writers.

Crime fiction has always held up a mirror to society. The Victorians were fascinated by sensational murder and the emerging science of detection; now we are obsessed with the forensic detail of violent death. And no other genre has so captivated and enthralled readers.

Vast troves of classic crime writing have for a long time been unavailable to all but the most dedicated frequenters of second-hand bookshops. The advent of digital publishing means that we are now able to bring you the backlists of a huge range of titles by classic and contemporary crime writers, some of which have been out of print for decades.

From the genteel amateur private eyes of the Golden Age and the femmes fatales of pulp fiction, to the morally ambiguous hard-boiled detectives of mid twentieth-century America and their descendants who walk our twenty-first century streets, The Murder Room has it all. 》》》

The Murder Room
Where Criminal Minds Meet

themurderroom.com

T0352494

Dorothy B. Hughes (1904–1993)

Dorothy B. Hughes was an acclaimed crime novelist and literary critic, her style falling into the hard-boiled and noir genres of mystery writing. Born in Kansas City, she studied journalism at the University of Missouri, and her initial literary output consisted of collections of poetry. Hughes' first mystery novel, *The So Blue Marble*, was published in 1940 and was hailed as the arrival of a great new talent in the field. Her writing proved to be both critically and commercially successful, and three of her novels – *The Fallen Sparrow, Ride the Pink Horse* and *In a Lonely Place* – were made into major films. Hughes' taught, suspenseful detective novels are reminiscent of the work of Elisabeth Sanxay Holding and fellow Murder Room author Margaret Millar. In 1951, Hughes was awarded an Edgar award for Outstanding Mystery Criticism and, in 1978, she received the Grand Master award from the Mystery Writers of America. She died in Oregon in 1993.

By Dorothy B. Hughes
(Select bibliography of titles published in The Murder Room)

The So Blue Marble (1940)
The Cross-Eyed Bear Murders (1940)
The Bamboo Blonde (1941)
The Fallen Sparrow (1942)
The Delicate Ape (1944)
Johnnie (1944)
Dread Journey (1945)
Ride the Pink Horse (1946)
The Candy Kid (1950)
The Davidian Report (1952)

Johnnie

Dorothy B. Hughes

An Orion book

Copyright © Dorothy B. Hughes 1944

This edition published by
The Orion Publishing Group Ltd
Orion House
5 Upper St Martin's Lane
London WC2H 9EA

An Hachette UK company
A CIP catalogue record for this book is available from the British Library

ISBN 978 1 4719 1735 6

www.orionbooks.co.uk

For Holly
who also writes mysteries

For Tony
who reads them

One

THERE WASN'T ANY SIGN saying this was it. Just like there wasn't any sign saying it was Friday night and May, a nice balmy night that didn't need any overcoat to bother you when you prowled. This was it all right. New York. The heart of New York. Broadway.

Three of them stood there, right in the middle of the sidewalk. They didn't pay any attention to the people walking at them and around them and away from them. They didn't even pay any attention to the babes digging them as they swished by. They stood there, Bill and Hank and Johnnie.

"This is the Great White Way," Bill announced.

"Don't look white to me," Hank said. "Kind of a dirty gray."

"It's the brownout," Bill told him. "We're in a war, soldier. Don't you know nothing, soldier?"

Johnnie said, "I want to ride on the subway."

The other two looked at him. Bill sighed. "There he goes again."

Hank stood five feet eleven and one half inches in his G. I. shoes. He had black hair and a big knuckly fist. He said "Pipe down, soldier."

1

Johnnie stood six feet two inches in his G. I. shoes. He didn't duck. But he winced. "I only said I wanted to ride on the subway."

Bill wasn't as tall as Hank but he was the one with the guide book to New York City in his head. Besides he'd already been here on one pass. He said, "Listen, Johnnie, in the first place you don't ride on a subway like on a merry-go-round. You ride in, like in a train."

"Choo-choo. Cat it, soldier?" Hank demanded. "You rode in a train all the way from Texas to New Jersey, didn't you? Didn't you? Now can't you pipe down?"

"I've never been on—in—a subway. I always wanted to ride on—in—one."

"Listen, Johnnie." Bill was patient. He planted himself in front of Johnnie, blocking more sidewalk, and Hank planted himself beside him. Johnnie looked down at both of them. They looked tough and they looked exasperated. All because he wanted to ride on a subway.

"Listen, we got to be back in camp by Sunday morning, don't we? We got thirty-three hours." Bill looked at his watch. "Thirty-two hours and forty-seven minutes. And time off that to get back to camp. We got just that long to see New York. And you want to ride in a subway!"

Hank snorted.

"I still do," Johnnie allowed. "Gee, I don't know what my dad and my mom and my kid sister and my kid brother would think of me if I came to New York and didn't ride on the subway. We used to talk about it all the time back home in Texas."

The two tough faces weren't weakening. No milk of human kindness dripping out. Johnnie changed tactics.

"Listen, why can't I ride on the subway while you guys go to the broadcast and the Stage Door Canteen and all the places you want to go?" He warmed up to it. "I'll just take me a little ride and then I'll meet you any place you say."

Bill looked at Hank. Hank looked at Bill. They looked at each other as if something smelled. They looked at Johnnie.

"You'll get lost," Bill said sternly.

Johnnie picked it up fast. "How can I get lost?" He argued, "You get on and you ride. You stay on and you come back where you started. All you got to do is get off where you got on. You can't get lost."

"You would," Bill stated.

"I couldn't." Johnnie had them wilting now. He stuck to his guns. "Even if I did, where do you think we are, Boona Boona? New Yorkers speak English, don't they? I could ask 'em, couldn't I?"

Hank put in his oar. "F'go'sakes, Johnnie, you don't mean you'd rather ride in a hole in the ground than go to the Stage Door Canteen? Dorothy Lamour might even be there."

"She lives in Hollywood," Johnnie told him.

"I saw her picture at the Stage Door Canteen," Hank declared. "Anyhow there's lot of girls there. Chorus girls!" He whistled. "Subway!" He snorted again.

"I still want to ride a subway. Gee, I don't know what Jimmie, my kid brother, would say if I couldn't tell him about riding on a subway—"

Bill interrupted. "Listen. Suppose we let you go. We're just wasting our time standing here flapping, Hank. Suppose we let you go and we mosey up to the

3

broadcast. Would you promise not to get lost? Would you promise to meet us in an hour at the Stage Door Canteen?"

"I promise," Johnnie grinned.

"And you won't buy the Brooklyn Bridge?"

"Do you think I'm a hick?" Johnnie demanded. "Don't answer that."

"Or the Empire State Building?"

He didn't deign a reply to that one.

"Where you got your folding dough?"

"In my shoe. Where'd you think?"

"How much in your pockets?"

Johnnie investigated. "Two dollars." He counted. "And ninety-seven cents. Four nickels, see?"

"Don't spend it all," Bill advised. "Now listen. It's seven twenty-two. You be at the Stage Door Canteen—no—" He looked at Hank. "He'll never find it." He turned back to Johnnie. "You meet us at the Astor, front door." He jabbed a finger in the black topcoat unfortunately passing them. "Scuse me. There it is across the street. See it. Astor. A-s-t-o-r. At nine o'clock. Don't be any later than that."

Hank said, "What a cluck. Sweating out the subway."

"You won't get lost?" Bill insisted.

"Don't worry about me." Johnnie grinned all over his face now.

"Nine o'clock, front door of the Astor."

Nine o'clock, the Astor, Johnnie repeated. His eyes weren't paying any attention to old Bill now. They were roving to the subway kiosk by the newspaper stand over there. People diving into the door and other people popping out of it. Like a magician putting rabbits

4

in a hat and pulling out chickens. He'd seen it happen once on the stage at the high school auditorium back home in Texas.

Hank had the last thing to say. He said it ruefully. "Tain't safe, Bill."

2.

Johnnie put his hands in his pockets, felt for a nickel, took a breath and dived into traffic. He made it to the island where the subway opening stood. He didn't bother to watch the departure of Bill and Hank. Couple of old women. Just because he'd got lost in Newark waiting for a train. That had been purely accidental. Just because Hank had been to school in Tulsa, he thought he was big time. Just because Bill was from Omaha, he thought he knew his way around any place. Well, he, Johnnie had been to Dallas a couple of times himself. And anybody could have got lost in Newark on Decoration Day. He wouldn't get lost tonight. There wouldn't be any parades tonight. If there were, he'd stand still and watch, not follow a baton twirler. He was bait for baton twirlers. Particularly blonde ones.

Johnnie kept his nickel in his hand as he ducked into the doorway. It wasn't so easy then. The subway wasn't standing on a track, waiting. He even had a sneaky feeling maybe Bill and Hank had been right after all. Maybe he shouldn't have wandered off from them. Maybe he was just a hick. That feeling didn't last. He found his way. He started down the stairs. He found where to drop a nickel. He went around corners and followed arrows and climbed up and down more stairs. He took his time, not like all these people darting around like polliwogs in a pool of water. He had plenty of time. A whole hour and a half before he had to meet the guys again. A whole hour and half to take a subway ride.

He finally reached the place where the subway train ran. Right under a big sign, black letters on white. Johnnie craned his neck to read it. Times Square. He was starting out from Times Square. All he had to do was come back to Times Square. A pipe. Johnnie was exceedingly content.

He stood there and observed a couple of trains. He didn't pay any attention to the three girls digging him. He wanted to get the full feel of a subway before he got on for a ride. Besides there'd be better looking girls at the Stage Door Canteen. He wanted to know what he'd look like when he was inside one of those trains. He wanted to know how about getting inside. He figured it out easy. When the door slid open you pushed in, no ticket or nothing. Then you grabbed a strap or sat on a wicker seat or leaned against the door after it slid closed. The train rumbled away out of sight down a long tunnel. He could go that far watching. When he was well filled with it, he moved up nearer the edge of the platform. He waited for the next train with the blissful anticipation of a small boy, and with only the slightest apprehension of something so radically new.

It was coming now. First you heard the roar. Then you saw the two green eyes, or the green and red eyes. Then the train rushed up, quieted, finally stopped moving. The magical doors opened. And Private Johnnie Brown walked inside, just as if he were used to subways.

The car was fair to middling crowded, not any sardine

in a can crowd, but enough so that Johnnie had to hold to a strap. He didn't mind that. It made it more fun than just sitting down. And the strap was easy on his hand; he didn't have to strain his seams like the five by five beside him. He got a kick out of watching the walls slide by, the lights blink, the jerk whenever the train stopped. It was like being in a movie. A movie of New York. He got such a kick out of it that he didn't pay any attention to all the other folks riding, most of them reading papers anyhow. He didn't even notice until past Columbus Circle that the pudgy guy beside him was talking German. When he first noticed it, he didn't rightly notice. It just seemed like part of being in a movie. Then he woke up that it really was German. Johnnie hadn't ever heard it spoken except in movies, movies about Nazis and spies, but he knew it was German all right. It was like listening to someone talk and clear their throat all at once.

He took a good look at the five by five then. A little fat fellow, about fifty maybe, with a moon face that should have had a handlebar mounted over the fat mouth. Maybe he had had one once; under his button nose the skin wasn't as weathered as on the cheeks and forehead. The man had on a dark suit and a pepper and salt topcoat. His black derby was too big for him; it sat down on his ears. Johnnie looked below to the fat man's shoes; you could usually tell whether a guy had folding money by his shoes. This one didn't have much. His feet were little and splayed out like a duck's. The shoes were black with pointed toes and even a shine wouldn't have made them look too good.

By that time Johnnie was catching some words, and

clear words like Munich, spitting out the ich, and Potsdam. There were other words that sounded like nothing at all. Totenkopfverbaede. Sicherheitsdrentl. Not Hitler. Maybe the fat man wasn't a spy after all. But he hadn't ought to be giving out with enemy flap. It just didn't sound good. Somebody ought to tell him it didn't sound good.

Johnnie had about made up his mind that he might say something to Pudgey when he happened to remember that the guy wasn't talking to him. And unless he was a nut, he wasn't talking to himself. The woman holding the strap on the other side of the man had a newspaper covering her face. She couldn't be it. That left the man sitting down in front of Pudgey. Johnnie took one look and knew that was the one. His face looked like he had indigestion or was about to have it; long thin nose, long thin cheeks, long pointed chin. His eye, the one Johnnie could see, was like a glass eye. No more expression than that. He was dressed better than the fat one. His derby fit him. His black overcoat had a velvet collar. Everybody in New York seemed to wear overcoats even if they didn't need them. This guy's feet belonged to him, the gray spats were clean and the black shoe tips had a high polish. His gray gloves were clean. He didn't look like the subway. Pudgey did. His fat hands had dirty fingernails.

The thin one wasn't doing any talking, just nodding every once in a while to show he wasn't a stiff, or maybe it was the subway that jerked his head. But the thin one could be a Nazi. If there'd been a monocle over that glass eye, Johnnie would have known he was one. He couldn't make up his mind about these two; he only knew they hadn't ought to talk the enemy language with a war on. The more hochs and achs and ichs he heard, the more it annoyed him. He had really made up his mind to say something when the car pulled up into another station. The fat man pushed to the door, the thin one stood up and followed him.

Johnnie followed both of them. He didn't think at all then, just like when he followed the parade in Newark. He simply walked on out the door after them.

He followed them up the soiled cement steps into the fresh air. When he got up there he didn't know what to do next or why he'd done this much. They'd crossed the street to the left, the near side, and were heading back downtown. The fat one was still talking.

Johnnie rubbed his ear. He didn't know what to do. He finally decided. Being as he'd gone this far he might as well finish it up. He'd tell that guy to stop talking German. They were half way down the block before Johnnie started loping after them. He could have caught up easy enough but his first spirit dwindled. What could you say to two perfect strangers, that is, in a nice way. Easy enough to tap old Pudge on his shoulder and say, "Listen, Bub. Speak United States. Don't you know we're in a war?" But that might spell trouble. And trouble was one thing Uncle Sam's uniforms were supposed to stay out of in the city. Sure as there'd be trouble, two M. P.'s, clubs and all, would pop out of the manhole cover and little old Johnnie Brown wouldn't be at liberty to see Grant's Tomb and the Statue of Liberty and the Empire State Building tomorrow. No, it had to be done in a polite way.

By now Johnnie knew it had to be done. He wasn't

taking this walk for the exercise. He'd walked enough in the last few months to last him a lifetime. Every time he thought about walking, his dogs started barking. Yet here he was walking on his pass and it wasn't going to be for nothing. Besides he'd have to have some excuse for being late at the Astor. If he hurried it up, maybe he wouldn't be late.

At that moment the small fat and taller thin turned left at the corner. Johnnie speeded up again. They'd crossed to the right of this street and were trotting past a row of houses, long, tall houses, each one exactly alike and each one looking like something out of an old fairy tale book. A whole street of fairy tale houses, with only little chinks of light showing under the window shades. Not very friendly looking. Johnnie slowed again. He might scare these guys if he went up now and tapped their shoulders. If someone pawed his back in the dark, he'd turn and slug. He looked over his shoulder quick but nobody was behind him. Quite a ways back was a guy cruising down the street minding his own business. That was all.

Johnnie faced front again. This time he heard it distinct. Hitler. The thin one was saying it, "Hitler," maybe even, "Heil Hitler." If so, Johnnie'd missed the Heil part of it. Hitler was enough. It made Johnnie mad. He was sure now these goats were spies and he knew he was going to do something about it. He was a soldier in the United States Army and if he was worth his salt he wasn't going to let a couple of Nazi spies walk around loose. He'd knock their heads together and drag them to the nearest police station. Two against one didn't bother him. He'd had some Commando training back at the camp in Texas. Besides he was bigger than both of them together.

While he was seeing red, the two men were climbing up the stone steps of one of the houses in the middle of the block. Pudgey was still talking while he pushed a doorbell. Before Johnnie could make it to the steps, the door opened a yellow streak. Pudgey said something. Someone inside made a sound like, "Errdorp." The guys went inside. The streak of yellow blacked out.

Johnnie walked on by. He marched past identical houses and then the street ended, like that. He turned right about face and marched back six houses; he'd counted them. There was only one thing to do. See if he could get inside that house. If he couldn't he'd at least get the street number. You couldn't see a thing from here on account of the brownout.

His G. I. boots clapped up the steps. He stuck his finger in the doorbell, left it there. Finally the yellow streak showed up again. Standing inside it was a pasty-faced young squirt with a red necktie on. Johnnie coughed. "Errdorp."

For a moment it didn't look as if it were going to work. The kid looked hard at him but he couldn't see much, peering out into the dark. Then he said, "Come in." He stepped aside.

Johnnie walked in. Just like that. He stood in a small hallway. There was one light in the ceiling, dark red carpeting on the floors, dark red paper on the walls. The staircase went right up a few paces from the front door. There was one straight chair in the hall, an old-fashioned hall tree against the staircase, and a green china umbrella stand at the foot of the stairs. There were four umbrellas sticking out of the umbrella stand. There wasn't a sign of a derby or a coat on the hall tree.

The squirt was giving Johnnie a good look now, a suspicious one. Mostly he was eyeing Johnnie's uniform. He didn't do so well on Johnnie's face. He had to crane up to it. He finally asked, part suspicion, part just plain wondering, "You are to see Herr Dorp?"

"Yeah," Johnnie said. Errdorp was either the fat guy or he was somebody that Pudgey was calling on. Either way it didn't matter.

"Wait here," Squirt said. He pulled aside the brown chenille drapes at the left and Johnnie went on in the parlor. He heard the squirt going up the stairs.

Johnnie felt fine as soon as he looked around the room. It reminded him of Aunt Clotilda's parlor up in Pampa. There was even a green velvet cover on top of the upright piano with little green balls of fringe dangling down over the music stand. There were old-fashioned plush-covered chairs, two of them rockers. There was a black sofa that looked hard as a rock and he bet it was. The chairs and sofa had crocheted doilies pinned on them. There was a worn red carpet all over the floor, with some scatter rugs over the wornest parts. He didn't kick them up to make sure but he knew he'd find loose threads if he did. Aunt Clotilda's carpet was that way. The chandelier hanging from the ceiling almost bopped him on the head when he walked under it. Four lights in it, converted from gas when electricity came in. And a gas fireplace under a golden oak mantel with a lozenge-shaped mirror set in it.

Johnnie stood in front of the mirror and stretched his mouth right and left. He smirked pretty and then he made his mouth an O. He jerked off his garrison cap. Mind your manners, soldier! He stuffed it in his pocket. He slicked back his yellow cowlick and said out loud, "Damn." Even a G. I. haircut couldn't take out all the curl. Didn't curl so bad down home except in summer when he got sweated. Back East with the ocean only a spit and a holler away, he couldn't keep it plastered down.

One thing in this room wasn't like Aunt Clotilda's. She had pictures of the family in big gold frames. Here there was a flower garden, and a castle on a river, and a sailing ship. All in nice bright colors. Johnnie turned back to the mirror. He wrinkled his nose. Then he stuck his right forefinger over his upper lip, puffed up his cheeks and squeaked, "Heil Hitler."

The folding doors at the back of the room took that particular moment to go click. Johnnie swung around. He was blushing like sixty. He knew it because even his ears were hot. A girl was digging him from the opening. Evidently she hadn't seen his imitation because she didn't look poisonous. And she certainly hadn't known he was in the room. If she had she wouldn't have stood there stock still with her big blue eyes flabbergasted on him.

She was a cute little half-pint. Her legs were covered up in gray slacks ending with saddle oxfords and butter yellow socks. Above the belt was a butter yellow sweater and she was built for sweaters. She had yellow curly hair and a face sort of like Sonja Henie. Not that cute. Not even Sonja Henie could be as cute as Sonja Henie looked. But this girl would come close to it.

She finally managed to get her mouth open. What

came out wasn't promising. She gaped, "What do you want?"

Johnnie might be cowed by the superior experience of his friends, Hank and Bill, but not by a babe. In fact he had a slogan, paraphrased, which he employed in dealing with all females who were not wives, mothers or grandmothers. It was: Never give a babe an even break. He smiled cheerfully at this member of the sex. He spoke with appreciation, "Hi ya, Babe."

She came into the room on that and she clicked the doors shut behind her. She hadn't paid any attention at all to his friendly advance. She was if anything more menacing than before. She demanded, "What are you doing here?"

He said, "I'm waiting to see Errdorp."

"Herr Dorp? Is he expecting you?"

"He ought to be. The Squirt"—he jerked his hand toward the hall—"went up to tell him ten minutes ago."

He had a small wince at the time lapse. Bill and Hank would get to the Astor first. They wouldn't like wasting time waiting. And Hank could be plenty tough. Johnnie took another gander at the babe and dismissed his conscience. They wouldn't wait long. They'd lost him before. He smiled his best at her.

She wasn't paying any heed. She was gasping again. "He couldn't. Herr Dorp is in conference." She put her eye on Johnnie. "Did Herr Dorp send for you?"

"Well, not exactly," Johnnie admitted.

"Who are you?" It wasn't any simple question. She was trying to figure out where she'd seen him before or what he was doing here or something.

He drew himself up. "I'm Johnnie Brown and no cracks about Harpers Ferry. I'm from Texas."

She demanded, "Why do you want to see Herr Dorp?"

Fat chance I'd tell you, sister, said Johnnie silently to Johnnie. This babe was just gunning for a chance to show him the door. He began, "We-l-l, there's something I want to talk to him about."

The girl pushed back her shoulders. The sweater fit even better that way. "Herr Dorp can't possibly see you tonight, Private Brown."

"Private First Class Brown," he interjected. "But you can call me Johnnie."

She went right on without a flicker. "He is very busy. If you will come some other time he would be glad to talk to you."

"Haven't got no other time," Johnnie told her. "My pass is only good until Sunday morning and I got a busy day lined up for tomorrow. Besides I'm a stranger. I'd never find my way back. I guess I'll just have to see him now. Won't take but a couple of minutes." He sat down on the plushy arm of the green chair.

She almost stamped a foot. "I tell you he can't see you. He is in a most important conference. He won't have time to see you."

Johnnie grinned. "Reckon I'll wait and see what Squirt has to say when he comes downstairs."

"Theo isn't coming downstairs," she stated firmly. "There's more important things for him to do right now."

"Did he tell Herr Dorp I was here?"

"He didn't get a chance to open his mouth. As soon

as he came in he was given instructions—" She did stamp her foot this time. "Why am I telling you all of this? It's nothing to you. Now will you please get out of here. Right now!"

Johnnie set the chair to rocking. "Who are you? Herr Dorp's daughter?"

"I am not."

"What's your name?"

"Will you please get out?" She softened just a little. "Believe me, I advise you to get out—now." She didn't say, "while you can," but it was almost on the tip of her tongue.

"Before you call the police?" he asked. He knew right away then that he wasn't going to get out until he had a heart to heart talk with this Herr Dorp. There was some hanky panky here. Even a guy from Texas could see that. The way her eyes jumped when he said, "police," and the way they looked quick to the brown chenille drapes. He looked too but nobody was peeking through them. He talked easy now, "Because if you want to, you just go right ahead and call them. There's nothing they can do to me. I didn't break in. The squirt —Theo—let me in." He looked under his eyes at her. "I'll even be pleased to tell the police what I want to talk to Herr Dorp about."

She put the tip of her tongue between her lips. "Why don't you tell me?" she coaxed. "If it's important I can take the message to Herr Dorp—" She broke off.

He'd heard the car too. She started on a run to the front windows. When she passed Johnnie she gave him a push back toward the sliding doors. "Get in there and don't make a light."

16

He didn't understand but he was used to taking orders. That was the Army for you. Especially orders from that top sergeant tone of voice. He backed to the doors, slid them, kept backing.

She was peeking between the window curtains. Her voice came muted but insistent over her shoulder. "Watch out for the—"

She didn't have to finish the sentence. She didn't have to tell him to watch out for the buckets. He'd found them. There was a noise like the house crashing down but it was only he and the buckets. Here in the dark he didn't know what he'd fallen into; he only knew it felt cold and gooey. He said all the swear words he knew.

She'd run back to him and she was adding her share. "I said, 'Watch out!' " she told him in disgust.

"Not soon enough," he complained. He picked himself up clammily.

She was gazing upward. "I guess they're too busy to investigate."

He took one step toward the light.

"Don't you come in here!" she warned. "Don't you track that stuff in the parlor!"

"What is it?"

"Paste," she said.

He recognized it now, smell and unpleasant texture. He shifted his feet. They felt as if he was standing in a mess of taffy.

"Thank heavens that car went by," she continued. "The paper hangers left their stuff. They didn't get finished this morning." She eyed him wearily. "Now what can I do with you?"

"If you'll tell that Herr Dorp—"

One ear cocked toward the window, she broke in. "Take off that suit."

He was alarmed. "I can't do that. It's against regulations."

"It certainly can't be regulations to walk around the streets drooling paste. Take it off."

He moved warily nearer the lighted room, gazed downward at the damage. He could feel it thick on his seat but he hadn't known that it also lay in gobs all over the front of his uniform. It had even splashed up on his tie. He didn't have words for what he was thinking. An M. P. would have them.

"Take it off," she commanded. "Quick."

"Then what?"

She shook her head dolefully. "I'll send it around to the little cleaner's on Columbus. He's open late. He can do something with it, I guess." She didn't sound too hopeful. "The shoes, too. He'll do them for me." She bristled. "Don't just stand there. Rudolph's due any minute. He has an awful temper when things go wrong." She raised her voice. "Take off that suit!"

"What'll I put on?" He just didn't know what to do.

"You can wrap yourself in one of those aprons the paper hangers left."

He wiped his hands on his pants, began unknotting his tie. This was against regulations. Only regulations didn't cover something like this. One thing, he wouldn't dare appear in public looking like a paste pot. The M. P.'s would pick him up for sure.

"Hurry," she urged.

"You tell that cleaner to hurry," Johnnie countered.

"I can't stick around here all night. I got big things to do."

"I'll get one of Dorp's men to take it around right away."

He had the shirt off, bent over to his shoes.

"Don't worry," she assured him, not a bit friendly, "I don't want you here any longer than necessary. In fact, I don't want you here at all."

He stepped out of the shoes into a dry place. His folding money was still safe in his sock. His fingers fumbled at his belt, hesitated. He gave her a look. "Aren't you going to turn around?"

She glared before she turned, then she ran back to the front windows. He heard the car as he stepped out of the gummy pants. He removed the wallet containing his identification papers. He removed his cigarettes, his matches, his Scout knife. She came running back to him. She caught his hand.

He pulled back. "Wait a minute. I don't have that apron—"

"Too late now. You're an idiot, but come on." She was pulling him and he understood it was important for him to cooperate, but fast. He wasn't dressed for company. He grabbed his stuff. She dragged him over to the chenille, stuck her head out, and hand-led him across to the staircase. She whispered, "Just don't talk. That's all."

He couldn't have talked if he'd wanted to at the moment. He was too loopy. He'd never run into anything like this before, not even in the movies. She didn't hesitate on the second floor but kept right on leading him, retracing the corridor soundlessly, up another flight of stairs to third. Her knuckles rapped on the door at the right, front.

"Who is it?" Another babe inside.

"It's Trudy. Open the door."

There were footsteps and the door opened, just a little. Trudy said, "I've got to dress fast. Rudolph's here." She pushed Johnnie inside. "For God's sake, do something with this!"

The door closed behind her. Johnnie was in a bedroom. Garbed only in striped magenta shorts, G. I. socks and dog tags, he was standing in a lady's bedroom. And before him was one of the most gorgeous queens he'd ever laid eyes on.

Two

THIS WAS MORE than a bedroom. It should be called a boudoir. It was all fluffy white and solid gold. Even the rugs were white. There was nothing in it that belonged to the shabby parlor below.

Trudy, the blonde number, had vanished completely. But this substitute was a honey. She was taller, slimmer, and had dark hair flowing down her shoulders. Her eyes were queer, narrow, and as green as grama grass. Her eyelashes stuck out about two feet, and her mouth and nails, even her toenails, were the color of strawberry jam. Johnnie started blushing when he took in the toenails. Because she certainly couldn't be called dressed. She had on a fluffy white thing that wasn't even fastened, and the white satin criss-crosses on her toes were what the kid sister called mules. Maybe this was one of those skin games he'd read about. Well, he wasn't going to give up his hard-earned pay for any racket. He'd dish out some Commando stuff first.

The green eyes weren't looking at him with any embarrassment or any particular surprise. She said, "You're late."

Johnnie blinked.

"Dorp's men were all supposed to be ready before seven. I don't know why Trudy put you off on me. I'm not dressed either. Is Rudolph actually here?" Her voice was kind of like sorghum, dark and thick, just a little foreign.

He began, "Well, a car stopped in front of the house and—"

She brushed his words aside. "Then I've a few moments. Rudolph wouldn't be in the first car." She studied him out of those slant green eyes. "Where's your uniform?"

"It had an accident," Johnnie admitted. She must have taken in his G. I. haircut and his dog tags to know he was a soldier. He wished she'd concentrate on the hair not the ensemble. His wallet and stuff didn't make much of a screen. He wished she'd offer him a bathrobe or a barrel.

"You look it." She frowned. "What are those strings around your neck?"

"Identification—"

"Dorp thinks of everything. Sometimes— What's your name?"

"Johnnie Brown." His toes curled on the white velvet rug.

"Johnnie. I'll slip up to the wardrobe and get you another suit. How tall are you? Come here."

He didn't want to but he moved toward her. She leaned against him. Her hair smelled like cape jasmine. The top of it touched his chin.

"Shoe size?"

"Nine and a half." This wasn't Johnnie Brown. He'd gone to sleep on the subway and he'd better wake up, but fast.

"Sit down. I'll be back in a moment." She trailed out, closed the door.

He didn't sit down. No irate husband was going to come barging in and catch him off guard. He kicked the gold leg of a chair and yelped, "Ow!" He wasn't asleep. He must be asleep. He rubbed his ear. He looked at his hands, went over to the gold and white dressing table mirror and squinted at the reflection. It was the same old face. Freckles on the long nose, red cheekbones, redder than usual, blue eyes, yellow cowlick that curled whether it was cut G. I. or Texas. He turned quick when the door reopened.

The beauty was back with a suit over one arm, black boots in one hand. She threw the clothes on the ruffled white bed, dropped the boots, closed the door and turned the key in it. "Put these on. There's no time to waste. Hurry."

He stood still in the middle of the floor. "You mean —I should get dressed here—in your room?"

Her strawberry red mouth curved in disdain. "If you're squeamish, go on in the bath. You need some soap and water anyway. That door. But hurry. They are here."

He picked up the clothes and the boots and went into the bath she'd pointed. It was all gold and white too. He had a feeling he hadn't ought to be doing this, putting on somebody else's clothes. There were Army rules about wearing uniform. But he didn't have a uniform at the moment and he certainly didn't want to go around in his underwear any longer. Not before strangers. Somehow this was like being in a game or a show, if it wasn't a dream. You did things you wouldn't think of doing in your right mind. The gal out there had an idea about something and this seemed to be it.

Sans pants and shirt, he called through the door, "Hey, what's your name?"

She said, "I am Magda. Hurry, Johann."

"Just plain Johnnie suits me, Princess," he called back. That was it; she spoke like a princess, gave orders like one. There was something peculiar about the whole setup. He could catch on that far. Two men talking German hadn't led him into any ordinary house. He might as well get dressed and find out some more. He lathered with the white perfumed soap, hands and face, dived for a towel that felt like velvet. Some dump this even if the girls vere kind of screwy. Black shirt, black britches, black coat with silver snakes embroidered on the collar, black leather Sam Browne belt.

He got into the britches. "What am I supposed to be, your chauffeur?"

"Never mind that. Hurry." She said something like: Damn my hair.

He got into the shirt, black tie, coat. He felt for his folding money, still there safe in the right sock. Boots a little big but better than too small. His wallet he slid into an inner pocket. Knife in his pants. Cigarettes handy. He started to open the door then remembered she was dressing. He called, "Can I come out now?"

"I wish you would. You'll have to hook my dress. I can't imagine where Trudy's vanished to."

He blinked when he saw her. She was something to pin up on the barracks wall. She'd piled her hair on top of her head and she looked more like a princess than ever. Her dress was all white skirts sprinkled with brilliants. A little piece of white covered her breasts. The white straps looked as if they wouldn't hold up a feather.

She pointed to the back end of the little piece of white. "There."

He swallowed.

"Hook it."

His fingers were too big, besides they jittered.

"Hurry," she commanded.

"I am hurrying," Johnnie mumbled. "These dang things are too small." He got it done somehow and heaved a sigh of relief.

Her green eyes examined him. "You'll do. Only stand up straight, like a soldier."

"I am a soldier."

"I know. Stand like this. Stiff. That's better. Where Dorp finds you young men, I don't know. Just remember to keep quiet and do as you're told, then you'll be all right. You carry my wrap, over your arm, like that, and my bag." She laid the white velvet cape just so over his left arm, thrust the white velvet purse in his hand. "You follow me. One moment—"

24

She went to her dressing table, opened a golden box, and pulled out a handful of stuff. Johnnie didn't whistle. His mouth merely pursed. She hung four bracelets on one wrist and three bigger ones on the other. The rocks in them would put out your eyes. On her ring finger she slipped a ruby, big as a reflector.

"Now. We won't wait for Trudy. She's probably been called downstairs. Come along and remember, don't speak unless you're spoken to. Ottomkopf is a terrible stickler for discipline."

"Yes, Princess," he grinned.

"And don't do that," she said sharply.

"Do what?"

"Don't smirk." Her green eyes were harassed. "Don't smile at all."

He grinned again. "Not just a little one?"

Her face was suddenly angry. "Do as you're told!"

"Okay, Princess," he said.

She seemed about to explode but she didn't. She only said, "Don't call me that," and she muttered, "Wait until I see Dorp. And Trudy."

He followed her to the staircase. She gathered her skirts and floated down with dignity, one hand just touching the balustrade. He followed, not so lightly. At the foot of the stairs she turned a warning glare. Then she smoothed it off until her face was a beautiful picture. She floated across to a double door. There were two guys outside it, one on each knob. One had yellow hair like Johnnie's, not curled, and one had brown hair. Neither one was as big as Johnnie. Their faces were screwed up tight, not a smile in a faceload. When Magda floated between them, the two acted like jumping jacks. They bowed to her and they bowed to each other and they swung open the door.

Not until he was following Magda into the room did Johnnie notice. Those guys had had on chauffeur suits just like his, even to the silver snakes on the collar. The reason he took notice then was because there were so many suits just like that already in the room. Otherwise he probably wouldn't have taken note; the room itself was knocking him loopy.

The first thing that hit him in the eyes were the three chandeliers. They were probably made of cut glass but they looked like big hunks of diamonds. The next thing he saw was Trudy and she was something to whistle at. She had on white skirts like Magda's but instead of brilliants there were ermine tails spotting them. The little white wisp above the waistline was even skimpier than Magda's. The hardware on her wrists was brighter than the chandeliers.

When he got his eyes off Trudy, Magda had already left him behind. He stuck out his boot to follow per orders but Trudy's bracelets were wig-wagging him to stand still. At least he gathered that was the signal. Anyway he stood still and watched.

Magda had floated up to a guy standing on a red velvet platform and she was curtseying to him just as if he were King of the May. He didn't look it. He looked like the squirt, Theo. Only he wasn't Theo. Theo was wearing one of the chauffeur suits with his face screwed up like the jumping jacks outside. As a matter of fact the King of the May had on one of the same kind of suits only his had a lot more silver embroidering it and there was a whole chestful of medals dangling on the front. This guy was a little taller than Theo but he had the same pasty face, the same patent leather hair. Johnnie figured it must be Rudolph, the one who had this house in such a tizzy.

Rudolph was smoking a cigarette in a three-inch long black holder with silver snakes on it. He gave Magda a nod then turned up his nose as if she smelled bad instead of like cape jasmine. Well, maybe he didn't like the smell of jasmine. Johnnie did. Reminded him of home, down around Corpus Christi way. Every man to his own smells.

By that time Johnnie had located Dorp. He was bursting the seams out of his white tie and tails. Probably rented it. His shoes still weren't good, the patent leather was wrinkled across the toes. But Dorp —at least Pudgey was Dorp to Johnnie till he found out different—looked happy. His fat face was bisected by a blissful smile. He was the only one in the room wearing a smile. The chauffeur squadron didn't even look human. And Dorp's pal, the glass-eyed, hatchet-faced menace, looked more sour than ever. He was standing beside Rudolph with a big ribbon across his middle, like pictures of the little New Year on magazine covers only the ribbon was red, and instead of a diaper he was wearing full dress like Dorp. His gray head looked as if it needed a shave.

This room was really something. The windows were covered with red velvet and all the chairs were red velvet. The one on the platform had a canopy of red velvet with a golden crown and scepter embroidered on it. Even the rug was red velvet. If he hadn't just come down the stairs with Magda, Johnnie wouldn't have believed he was in the same house he'd entered half an hour ago. This room and Magda's room certainly didn't fit with Aunt Clotilda's parlor downstairs.

Magda came out of the curtesy just as if she were used to making one every hour on the hour. She pulled out all the stops in her voice. It throbbed. "Rudolph, I cannot believe you are here at last. You must tell me all of your travels, all the excitement. But you are tired, my dear—"

"I'm not tired," Rudolph put in. He had an adenoidal tenor. "And there wasn't any excitement."

"Ah, but your escape!"

"It was dull." Rudolph's lip pouted. "I thought it would be exciting." His beady black eyes glared at the man beside him. "But it wasn't. Herr Ottomkopf put me on the plane in Mexico City. I flew to El Paso."

"You just come from El Paso?" Johnnie burst out happily. He ceased. The way everyone in the room turned on him he might have been announcing that he had a bad case of cholera. "Well," he began in explanation.

Magda was ice. "Quiet," she commanded. "I'm sorry, Rudolph."

Dorp's hands waggled. He spoke English now but so thickly he reminded Johnnie of Captain Katzenjammer. "I regret, Your Highness. I regret much, but the draft it takes so many of our young men and we must train more, sometimes with such little time." His voice oozed away under Rudolph's empty stare. The silence was so rugged that Johnnie could feel his ears sizzling.

Rudolph's adenoids began again. "From El Paso I

had to come by train. Unendurable!" He fanned his face with the cigarette holder. He had a big ruby on his finger, too. Johnnie never had liked guys who wore jewelry. He knew for certain he wasn't going to like Rudolph. Highness or no highness, let Rudy make one crack about Texas and he'd pop him one. But Rudolph didn't. He jabbed the cigarette at the glassy-eyed man beside him. "If you could come by plane, Herr Ottomkopf, why must I endure days on the filthy train?"

Ottomkopf bowed. "For safety, Your Highness." He had a worse accent than Herr Dorp. "I have explain. The incognito—"

"I didn't like it," Rudolph said, and the steel spine of Ottomkopf wobbled just a trifle.

Magda poured oil. "It's all over now, Rudo. From now on you travel by plane, the best planes. Dinner is prepared. Shall we—"

"I'm not hungry," Rudolph said petulantly. He popped his cigarette holder like a water pistol. The stub fell to the carpet. Herr Ottomkopf with no expression picked it up. He passed it to the black suit next to him. That guy passed it on. Johnnie never did see who finally swallowed it. He was looking at Trudy again. Cute as a button, a Sonja Henie button, she was. But she was on pins and needles about something. It was making her blue eyes jump around. It couldn't be that she was jealous of Magda taking over the great Rudo. Nuts to that.

Herr Ottomkopf fitted another long white cigarette into the long black holder. He struck a match. Nobody made a false move until the ritual of His Highness' cigarette was over and the first blast of smoke exhaled.

Magda smiled. "We have your favorite foods prepared, Rudolph. I remembered each one." Johnnie wasn't too dumb to catch that glint on Trudy's face. She'd done the remembering, not the gorgeous Magda. "Wienerwurst. Head cheese and pickled walnuts. And apple cake and champagne."

"I'm not hungry." Rudolph repeated. "I ate at the station."

Everyone glared now at the Number One boy next to Ottomkopf. He snapped his heels and, without relaxing his face, recited, "It is true. His Highness wishes to eat. He eats. I remain with him."

"I was hungry then," Rudolph explained loftily. "I'm not hungry now. I had a bowl of chile con carne and a double chocolate malt."

Johnnie winced. The junk they called chile in any eating house east of Kansas City was slop for the pigs.

"Now I'm going to Ruprecht's party," Rudolph announced.

That one really threw them. The big shots actually moved from their invisible chalk marks on the red rug. Big stop signs were written all over their faces but nobody yelled, "No."

Magda finally cried, "You can't do that!"

Johnnie found out then why everyone had kept quiet. Rudolph's face turned to a regular neon sign, half green, half red. Furthermore it took on the look of a particularly mean little oaf who had a mud ball in his fist and no one near enough to disarm him. He closed his mouth tight and said nothing.

Dorp began dripping, "What she means, Your Highness, is that with all the risks we have took, it is not wise you leave mine house until time we go to the Clipper."

"I'm going to Ruprecht's," Rudolph stated nastily.

"It's impossible." Trudy was tiny but she stepped right up to him. "Ruprecht himself agreed that it was wiser if he didn't try to see you. We'd have had him here otherwise. But the danger of him being followed—the F. B. I. follows him night and day."

"Ruprecht's at a party," Rudolph said. "I'm going too. I'm invited."

"He doesn't even know you're here!" Dorp's face was full of little rivulets running down into his fat neck.

"He does too," Rudolph countered. "I telephoned him."

"You telephoned him!" This time they were kicked in the teeth. They turned balefully as one man on the Number One boy.

He didn't flinch. He clicked his heels and recited, "It is true. His Highness wishes to phone. I remain outside. He phones."

"And did you think of the F. B. I. waiting to apprehend His Highness?" Dorp shouted. "Did you not know you were to come direct to headquarters from the train?"

Rudolph mused, "When I want to do something, I do it. I want to go to Ruprecht's party. And nobody's going to stop me." He stuck out his chinless chin at the whole roomful.

That stymied them. All but Trudy. She said, "Don't be an ass, Rudolph. Ruprecht isn't alone. He's a guest of Lessering."

"I know it. Ferenz Lessering is my friend." Rudolph

blew smoke. "I owe him one hundred fifty thousand rudls. Or rather the kingdom does. He'll be glad to see me." His eyes popped. "And I'm not an ass, Trudy."

"You are if you do anything so utterly, utterly—"

"Icky," Johnnie supplied.

"Quiet!" Magda yelled. She turned back to Rudolph. "Don't you see it's a trap? It must be a trap. Ruprecht agreed—"

"You're all being revoltingly stupid," Rudolph said. "I am going to Ruprecht's party right now. I like parties. The Clipper doesn't leave until morning. It is not yet eight o'clock. What do you expect me to do until tomorrow? Sit and eat wienerwursts!" He shuddered. "Janssen!"

The Number One jumping jack clicked again.

"My coat."

"If you insist on seeing your brother," Herr Ottomkopf gritted, "I will attend you."

"And I," Herr Dorp sighed.

"Of course, I'll go with you, Rudo," Magda purred. "If you really need to see Ruprecht so badly."

Johnnie looked for Trudy to make it a quorum. Somehow she'd slipped out of the room. Probably while he was watching Janssen perform.

Rudolph drew himself up but he didn't protest. Janssen helped him into a black coat that buttoned under his chin. Janssen put on the patent leather hair a black dress cap, officers' cap. Johnnie frowned. He hadn't caught it before. These weren't chauffeur suits; they were soldier suits. But not of the U. S. Army. His stomach teetered for the first time.

Dorp said, "Wait. Theo, you will come with me. We

must have coats for the men. They cannot go into the street this way." He paddled out. Theo goose-stepped after him.

Magda turned. "My cape. Johann! *Johnnie!*"

"Who, me?" He'd been watching Rudolph pop another butt to the floor.

"Yes, you."

He brought it to her, laid it about her shoulders. She looked daggers but she wouldn't stab him in front of the great Rudolph. She pulled the hood over her head, took the velvet handbag, fumbled in it. "My gloves. One moment, Rudolph. I forgot them." Her smile would melt butter. She swirled, made swiftly out the door.

Johnnie turned, followed her. She was almost at the head of the stairs before he started up. But he had his orders. Follow me. He hesitated just a minute before he opened the door of her room. Gloves might mean something like powder my nose. Just the same he went in. He wanted a word alone with her. He couldn't go out on the street like this. What if the M. P.'s spotted him?

He nearly backed out again fast. She was standing in front of her fancy dressing table. And she was just putting a little blunt-nosed shiny gun into the velvet purse.

2.

Magda saw his reflection in the dressing-table mirror. She whirled her white skirts. The velvet bag was closed now. "What are you doing here?" she demanded.

He found his voice. "You told me to trail you, Princess." He burst out with it. "What are you doing with that gun?"

She held the velvet against her. She spoke carefully. "I think this is a trap. There are certain people who do not want Rudolph to return to his country." She flared, "How dare you question me?"

"Where is his country?"

She had a pair of long white gloves and she began easing them over her wrist diamonds. "Did you ever hear of Luxembourg?"

"No'm."

She was impatient. "Well, it isn't Luxembourg but it's near there. If you've never heard of it, the name wouldn't mean anything."

He was suspicious. "Not Germany?"

"No, not Germany," she snapped. "Come along. I wouldn't trust that idiot not to go off and leave me here."

"Listen, Princess," he began.

"Come along," she commanded, shoving past him. "And I told you to stop that Princess stuff."

She made time on the stairs but she didn't get away from him. The others were gathered in the second floor corridor. The soldiers had black coats covering up their uniforms. Dorp was giving orders with his fat fingers. The nails were still dirty. "You will go in this car—you in that—"

Magda stated, "I, of course, will go with Rudolph." She gave him the big smile, put her hand under his arm.

Trudy shoved a coat at Johnnie. "Put this on. Button it up." She had a little short cape of ermine around her shoulders.

"I can't go with you," Johnnie told her under his breath. "Not without my uniform. Where's my uniform?"

"It isn't back yet," Trudy muttered. "You look all right. You might as well come along. I might need you. And it'll be a good party."

Rudolph whined, "What are we waiting for? It's a supper party."

"You stick with Magda," Trudy ordered under her breath. "You're her attendant." Johnnie didn't get to say any more. She slid back to Dorp and Theo, started with them down the stairs.

The squadron stood at attention on either side. The two men who had been outside the throne room followed Dorp, Theo and Trudy. After them went Ottomkopf and Janssen, Magda and Rudolph, with Johnnie bringing up the rear. He didn't know what else to do. If he lost sight of Trudy he might never get his uniform back. He hoped the brownout was still working. It'd be too bad if the M. P.'s spotted him now.

There were no strangers visible in the street. Two cars stood at the curb. The first was a Chevrolet sedan. One jumping jack was at the wheel. Theo climbed in beside him; Dorp and Trudy took the rear. The big black limousine behind it had the other jumping jack in the driver's seat. Ottomkopf took his place beside him. Magda and Rudolph took up the back seat. That left jump seats for Janssen and Johnnie.

The cars rolled away. Johnnie took out his package of cigarettes. "Smoke?" he offered Janssen.

Janssen said sharply but softly, "No!"

Johnnie lit his own. Janssen looked horrified. He was

making gestures but Johnnie ignored them. If they meant that Johnnie shouldn't have a cigarette that was too bad. Rudolph was smelling up the car with his brand. And Rudolph was complaining, "I don't know that I like this plan at all, Magda."

"You want to reign, don't you?"

"Yes, certainly I do. That's the only reason I left Mexico. I wasn't afraid of those men Otto was always burbling about. I never laid eyes on them. I liked Mexico. I learned to eat chile. I dearly love chile, Magda. Who's going to make chile for me at home?"

"Chile." She almost snorted it. "With a throne waiting."

"I came, didn't I? But I don't like it. How do we know it's safe?"

"The enemy can't last another year, Rudolph. You'll have to be on hand to take over, near, where you can fly over the border in a couple of hours."

"How do I know it isn't just a trick to get me back there? Who is this dreadful little fat man, Herr Dorp, anyway? Where did you find him? How do we know he isn't working for Hitler, trying to get me to go back and be a puppet king? I won't be a puppet king. I'll run away again. That's why I ran away before."

"And because you didn't like the bombs," she slurred.

"And no butter and no sugar and no coffee. In Mexico—"

Magda's voice was sweet as molasses but underneath there was that glint she showed when she talked to Johnnie. "You want to be king, don't you? If you aren't there when the enemy is defeated, the people will elect

a president. How would you like to see your stable-
man, Kraken, president?"

Johnnie leaned around to put in his oar. "Abraham
Lincoln was born in a log cabin. He made a good president."

"Who asked you?" Magda retorted. Her green eyes
widened in disgust. "How did you get in this car?"

"I'm following you," Johnnie said. "Like you told
me."

"I wanted you left behind. You're stupid. I meant
to tell Dorp." She shook her head. "That's what comes
of hurrying, upsetting everything."

"I didn't want to come. That's what I wanted to
tell you upstairs. I have to—"

"Keep quiet," she ordered.

"Okay, Princess." He sighed back to the front.

"You are speaking to the Duchess Magda!" Rudolph
thundered. Only it came out a squeak not a thunder.
"Who is this oaf, Magda?"

"I'm no oaf." Johnnie swung back again with his
fist doubled. "I'm Johnnie Brown of Texas and if you
know what's good for you, you'll button up your lip
with that oaf stuff. Before I paste you one—"

Janssen had swung to face him. His hand might have
been on a gun. It was in his pocket.

Magda spoke quietly. "No violence, Janssen. Remember, we're in New York."

Rudolph squeaked, "This fellow—he is threatening
me—me!"

Magda apologized. "It is unfortunate. I will tell Dorp.
So many new men, untrained. He will be disciplined."

Johnnie had a mouthful more to say but the car was turning in a gate now. Two men on guard were talking to the chauffeur. Johnnie looked out the window. He could see the silver of a river below. Must be Riverside Drive, he figured. He'd seen pictures of it in the New York Sunday papers. This big house set back from the street was evidently one of the few relics of days when New Yorkers lived in homes. All around it were towering apartments.

The car passed inspection. It followed the smaller lead sedan up to the porte-cochere. Magda spoke to Johnnie as he waited to help her out of the car. Her face was frozen. "If you have any sense at all, you will keep quiet."

Johnnie put out his chin which was far from chinless. "I'll keep quiet so long as that false alarm doesn't start any more of that oaf business. I'm an American and no tin horn prince is going to shove—"

She didn't wait for him to finish. Rudolph had been unpacked by then. She left Johnnie with only a baleful green glare to remember her by. He took a lungful of air and followed.

A real butler opened the door, knee britches, silver tray on his hand, and all the fixings. Dorp must have arranged things. The butler didn't ask for tickets. The entrance hall was massive with broad marble stairs leading to a marble balcony. Johnnie goggled. He'd never even imagined anything like this. It was a regular palace. From above there was music and chitter chatter. The butler took all the wraps, handed them around to a flock of knee-britched assistants. He led the way up the marble stairs.

Johnnie was right on Magda's heels. He hoped there would be a place to sit down upstairs. He was getting tired of standing on his feet. Enough of that at camp without wasting a free night that way. The butler disappeared when they reached the balcony. Some of the party milling about there looked pretty curious at them. Johnnie didn't wonder. It wasn't a fancy dress ball but this bunch looked it. He eyed the marble benches along the wall but he couldn't make a break for it as yet. The yellow velvet cushions were tempting.

The man who came out of the ballroom door weighed about two hundred and ninety pounds, but he stood six feet two in his stocking feet. He was that much taller than Johnnie. He had a face all pouches, a prissy mouth, thin brown hair and a voice like a high school girl's. "My dear Rudolph," he burbled. "This is an honor." He fussed with his white tie while he talked. "Magda, my love, how sweet of you to decide to come!"

"Ruprecht invited me," Rudolph said nastily. "The others insisted on coming too."

"But I wanted them. I love them." His great arm enveloped Rudolph's shoulders. "Now where can Ruprecht be?"

"He's over there, Ferenz," Trudy pointed.

The guy at the end of her finger was on a bench at the far corner of the balcony. He was the one doing a little smooching with the platinum blonde babe.

"That's Ruprecht," Magda agreed with acidity.

"Let me fetch him." Ferenz' tails switched half way to the bench before Ruprecht looked up. When he looked up, he grinned. He was one of the best-looking guys Johnnie had ever seen. He looked like a movie actor, the kind the babes went all out for. Maybe like Alan Ladd. Tall, almost six foot, blond, blue-eyed, and poured into his full dress suit.

He left the babe flat and ambled past Ferenz to the group. "Hiya, Rudo," he called. He was a little popped, maybe more than a little. He swayed when he clapped his brother's shoulder and he held on to it. "See you brought the family." He unloosed Rudy and beamed on Magda. "Hiya, Beautiful." He pinched Trudy somewhere for she jumped and said, "Ow." "Hiya, Toots. Well, I didn't think old sourball Otto would let you come but here we all are together. That calls for a drink." He pulled Rudolph to the wide doors.

Ferenz lisped anxiously. "Wait a minute, Rupe. Just a minute, dear. When Shanks informed me that Rudolph was here, I arranged a little—" His face relaxed. There was a roll of drums as he was speaking. He nodded his head beatifically as the butler trumpeted, "His Royal Highness, Prince Rudolph of Rudamia!" There were gasps, applause, and a lot of craning toward the balcony. "Her Royal Highness, Princess Ermintrude of Trudamia. Her Highness, Duchess Magda of Trudamia."

"And entourage!" Ruprecht murmured. Entourage was a good fifty-buck word but it didn't throw Johnnie. He was already thrown by Trudy stepping out on Ferenz' arm. She should have looked like a midget hanging there but all of a sudden she really looked like a royal highness. She must have done this kind of performance before. The band struck up some kind of a march. The party, led by Magda and Rudolph, set out. Johnnie followed. But as soon as the others were surrounded by simpering women and bowing men, Johnnie ditched the parade. He'd seen the buffet over at the right. He sashayed straightaway toward it. He hadn't known for some little time what those funny feelings were in his stomach. Now he knew. Food. The hamburgers he and Bill and Hank had put away at six o'clock weren't exactly a full meal. This mess was a hungry guy's heaven. Turkey and hams and a big pink rib roast, dishes full of everything.

Johnnie heaved a plate at one of the gold buttons behind the table. "Fill 'er up," he suggested. From then on all he had to do was nod while Gold Buttons pointed to this and that and this. When there were about three layers he said, "Hold it." He could come back for seconds, no rush for chow here. Everybody was too busy babbling around the royal entourage. Johnnie gathered up a napkin and a handful of silver. Big white napkins, the kind Mom had for company dinners back home. With a couple of fingers he managed to balance a cup of coffee. Three lumps of sugar, and cream you could cut with a knife. Ferenz must be (a) a farmer, (b) a hotel, (c) a hoarder in a big way.

Nobody paid any attention to Johnnie when he walked out of the room. There wasn't anyone on the balcony now. Johnnie picked the couch down below where Ruprecht had had the platinum babe cornered. He sort of wished the babe had been left over. But he didn't need her now. He dived into supper. When he'd worked his way through the first two layers he had time to think. He wanted to think. It was essential that he think. Because he wasn't asleep. He'd never fed this well in a dream.

Being awake the first question was, how had he come to get mixed up in this screwy business? He was a little embarrassed by that one. He was always getting mixed up in something. Like the time in San Antonio when he—he blushed above his ears. No sense getting side-tracked. That babe had been a honey. But there were no flies on Trudy. On Magda neither, if she'd just stop pawing over Rudo, the goon, and be human. Cut out the girl angle. What was it all about?

Well, they weren't Nazis. Because they were waiting for Hitler to hit the banana peel and he for one hoped they were right about it going to be soon. He'd like to finish up this war fast and get back home to Texas. On the other hand why were they scared of the F. B. I. if they weren't Nazis? And why did Dorp talk German to Ottomkopf in public? And what about this royal high-ness stuff? Who were they trying to kid?

Maybe the big fat nancy who ran this swell dump. Maybe they were putting on the dog to crash this party. Maybe, Johnnie considered with blissful excitement, maybe they were society jewel thieves! The bliss faded. Couldn't be. Because none of them wanted to come to the party except Rudolph.

Wait—a—minute! He doubled back to his plate. Would the dolls have dressed up like Christmas to sit home and eat wienies in Dorp's house? Uh uh. They *said* they didn't want to come to the party. Johnnie's head nodded sagely. What quicker way could they get Rudolph to agree to coming than to balk him?

The guns Magda and Janssen carried. The soldiers left behind, but each one hatted and coated for the street. They were probably outside now surrounding

42

the joint. They would have had to come by subway because there were only two cars. Couldn't be very big-time crooks with only two cars. Well, if there was any trouble he'd stick to Ruprecht. That Ruprecht looked like a good Joe. Tight or not you could tell that. The others—well, maybe Trudy was okay but the rest he wouldn't trust as far as he could heave a jeep. As for pasty Theo and the goon, he definitely didn't like them at all.

Johnnie rubbed the last hunk of roll over his plate, tucked it in his mouth and chewed. The trouble was he couldn't afford to get mixed up in any trouble. He was in the Army now. The C. O. simply wouldn't understand that it was purely accidental. He let out a well-filled sigh. He'd better go in and corral a few chocolate éclairs, then get going. He'd never be missed. And a piece of that strawberry pie and another cup of coffee. His uniform ought to be back from the cleaners by now.

He sat up suddenly. He couldn't get going! He didn't know where to go. He didn't have any idea how to get from here to Dorp's house. That's what he got for arguing with Rudolph in the car instead of watching the scenery. There was one thing he could do. Ask Trudy where the house was. He anticipated a little trouble on that count. Trudy wanted him here. She'd said she might need him. Well, he wasn't going to act as any stupe for jewel thieves.

Better ask Magda.

Better have the éclairs first. There might be a rush on them before he pried Magda loose from Rudo and got through wrangling with her. She reminded him of the kid sister. She'd rather argue than eat. Only Sis didn't tell him to keep quiet and her eyes weren't grama-grass green. He sighed again. He wished he were back home in Texas. But he perked up. Mom and Dad and the rest of the folks would get a big boot out of his being at a Lessering's party. If that guy was one of the Lesserings.

He stacked his dishes and cased the inside of the ballroom before entering. He didn't want to be bothered by any more orders until he had dessert. He never really felt comfortable after a meal until he'd had dessert. Preferably a chocolate dessert. Or strawberry. No one seemed to be looking for him. He went back to the cafeteria. A couple of others had found it by now but none of the royal highness bunch.

"More?" asked the gold buttons with the yon-Cassius look. Johnnie had learned that flap from Bill. It meant scrawny.

Johnnie didn't like the way the guy said it but there wasn't any point in starting trouble with the boss of the supply train. "I've had enough of that junk," he scowled. Then he smiled. "Now I want dessert. That one." He pointed to the biggest chocolate éclair. "And some strawberry pie." He'd missed the caramel éclairs on his first foray. "And that one. And another cup of coffee."

He made it out on the balcony without being spotted, headed back to his chosen spot. He tried the pie first. Real strawberries! And whipped cream, an inch thick. Curiosity was biting him worse than the need for food. Where was this Luxembourg? And where were Rudamia and Trudamia? If Bill were here, he'd know. Or he'd look it up in the Base library. Trouble with Johnnie was he'd never taken much to schooling. But he'd played right end two years with Texas A. and M. Bill hadn't done that even if he did know Shakespeare like it was a book.

Johnnie sampled the chocolate éclair. Look it up. He could look it up himself. A house this big and fancy would be sure to have a dictionary. He took his plate and cup and made his way to the marble stairs. Below there were several of the knee-britched fellows marking time. The one Johnnie approached was bow-legged as a cowhand.

"Have you got a dictionary?" Johnnie asked.

"Yes, sir. This way, sir."

He trailed along to a room at the left beyond the staircase. The flunky opened the door. "The library, sir. You will find the reference works over there, sir." Over there was just a couple of miles away down the room.

"Okay," said Johnnie. This room had more books in it than the Carnegie library back home. They were stacked on shelves from the floor to the high ceiling. Bill would sure go for this library. Even Johnnie did. There was a real fire burning in the fireplace. Soon as he took a look at the dictionary—it wouldn't be the dictionary, he knew better than that, it would be the encyclopedia—he'd stretch out on the couch by the fire for a smoke. Meantime he'd better look up those places while he had a chance. He didn't take to this flying blind.

There were plenty of high-backed velvet chairs pulled up in front of the shelves. Each one had a reading stand beside it with a little pin-point light attached. It didn't look as if you could read by such a little light but it worked fine. Johnnie pulled out Lu, Ru, and Tr; stacked them beside him. His plate and coffee he set on the reading stand. That worked fine too. He lifted Ru to his lap. While he was thumbing for Rud, he finished the strawberry pie.

The door at the other end of the room was opening softly. Johnnie froze. When he had the nerve he peered around the back of his chair. Magda was closing the door even more softly. He ducked back again fast. He didn't want her catching up to him, bossing him around, not until he'd finished eating. Evidently she didn't see him because she didn't say anything. The back of his chair was to the door and the coffee cup shaded the pin-point. He took another cautious peek. She was standing in front of the fire, her back to the reference corner, facing the door.

Carefully Johnnie took up the chocolate éclair in his fingers, bit off a hunk. He didn't have to chew; it melted in your mouth. Magda was waiting for some-one. She didn't wait long. The door opened again, not so carefully. Johnnie didn't dare take a glimpse just yet. Anyone coming in the door could see him if he stuck his neck out. He didn't need a look. He knew the voice. It was the only male voice he'd heard tonight that he'd want to hear again. It was Ruprecht.

Johnnie heard him close the door and walk over toward the fireplace. He was saying lazylike and still kind of tight, "What's the game, Gorgeous? Psst, meet me in the library at midnight."

46

Johnnie took a quick one at his watch. It wasn't midnight. It wasn't even ten o'clock.

Magda said, "Oh, Ruprecht!" She sighed. She was putting it on thick for him. "I had to see you. I had to explain to you."

"Explain what?" There was a click, click. Johnnie peered fast. Ruprecht had set two quart bottles of champagne on the table by the couch.

"Ruprecht, please."

"Don't be a ninny, Magda. It's worked, hasn't it? Dorp smoked out Ottomkopf. Otto smoked out Rudolph. You've the Rudamian ring right now on your stunning finger, sweetheart. What is there to explain? Nary a hitch. How about a little toastie?"

"Ruprecht!"

Johnnie ducked back fast. He took a bite of éclair, a big one. That was the glint in the voice. But she didn't follow it up with a bawling out. There was silence, so much silence he could hear himself swallowing chocolate custard. Maybe they were sneaking up on him right now. He crammed the last end of éclair in his mouth and, braving it, peeked. He almost choked. You couldn't have wedged a hair off Magda's head between those two!

He couldn't move. That was a clinch that was a clinch. And the kiss that went with it could have taught Gable and Turner plenty. But Johnnie wasn't the only appreciative audience.

In the doorway stood Trudy.

3.

Trudy didn't look particularly surprised, nor particularly angry. She was just plain disgusted. She ought to have coughed or something to let on to the hot cargo that she was present. Of course, so should he, Johnnie, but that was different. He hadn't barged in on them; he was here first. The strain was getting him. Something had to break up that clutch. If Magda didn't open her eyes pretty soon and see that look on Trudy's mouth, he'd drop the encyclopedia and take the consequences.

He relaxed when Trudy said one word. "Cut."

Ruprecht beat Magda to it. He swung around as if he'd been kicked in the pants. Magda just tossed back her head and ran her hands down her hips. Johnnie didn't whistle. He chewed.

Ruprecht said, "For God's sake, Trudy. You should be belled."

Trudy didn't pay him any heed. She kept her eyes on Magda. Her mouth was curled up. "I thought I'd find you here. And I thought you'd be at it."

Magda said, "Sneak."

"Rudolph is waiting for you. He's going to make a speech." Her little smile wasn't friendly. "Hand in hand with his betrothed. You'd better snap out of it. Maybe Rudolph can't make with the pash like Rupe but he is the oldest. And he doesn't like to be kept waiting."

Magda begged eagerly, "You mean he's going to announce—"

"At Ferenz' special request. And you'd better get that kissed look off your mouth. Rudolph is dumb but not that dumb."

Magda remarked while she did repair work, "You're a nasty little twirp and you always were." She replaced the mirror and lipstick in her purse. "See you later,

Rupe." She sailed out of the room like a queen on a hurry call.

Trudy stood aside for her to pass. She made a good Bronx sound before Magda was out of the doorway. The way she slammed the door after her nearly jiggled the book off Johnnie's lap.

"Now see here, baby mine," Ruprecht began.

Trudy stomped. "I'm not your baby. Definitely not. I knew you'd wolf after almost anything in skirts but I did think you'd draw the line at that one."

"Now, honey."

"And don't honey me!" Trudy shouted. "Honey her. I don't care. You know she's a no-good slut but if that's what you want you can have it. All I want is to know why you invited Rudo here tonight."

"I didn't."

"You did. After you promised you'd stay out of the picture. You swore to me you wouldn't try to see him."

"I swore I didn't want to see him. I still don't. He makes me sick to the entrails. And you swore you'd keep him out of my sight. Then the whole passel of you escort him here with a guard of honor."

"You invited him."

"I did not, baby mine."

"He phoned you. You said come to the party. You knew he wouldn't turn down a party. Has he ever?"

"Where do you get such silly ideas, Toots?"

"From Rudo himself."

"He's a filthy liar. He always was."

"Yes? How would he know there was a party at Furry's house if he hadn't phoned you from the station? He just got in tonight. He's been on a train for days.

How could he know if you didn't invite him to come?"

Johnnie had forgotten caution. He watched this openly, caramel éclair in hand and mouth. It looked as if she'd pop Rupe any minute. She was mad enough. And she was closing in.

"I give you my word, Trudy. He couldn't have called me. I was with some friends at Twenty-One. I didn't get back here until the party was started." He decided, "It must have been Furry who invited him. I didn't have a chance to chat with him until you and yours barged in."

"Ferenz wouldn't. He refused to put up the money to bring Rudolph to New York unless Dorp promised he shouldn't have to lay eyes on him. He wouldn't invite him."

"He would if Rudo called up and announced himself. You know Furry. Etiquette. Didn't you have anyone watching Rudolph?"

"Janssen."

"That robot. Where was Otto?"

"He'd come up to the house earlier with Dorp to make last arrangements. Rupe, we've got to get Rudo out of here."

Ruprecht was lighting a cigarette. "Take him, my little love. I don't want him."

"You'll have to help. And I'm not your love. What are *you* doing here?"

That last question wasn't to Ruprecht. It was delivered with gusto and without pleasure. Johnnie spoke through his éclair. "Who me?"

"Who else?" She came around, Ruprecht following,

until she stood in front of Johnnie. He couldn't get to his feet without dropping the encyclopedia on hers. He just sat there.

"What are you doing here?"

"I'm reading the encyclopedia." Johnnie's dignity was marred by the mouthful of goo. "At least I was," he swallowed. "I was before the row started."

"Who's he?" Ruprecht pointed. "One of Dorp's men?"

"Yes," Trudy said.

"No," Johnnie said.

A discreet knock on the door ended that one. After the knock came Theo. He made a jerky bow. "His Royal Highness wishes you upstairs in the ballroom."

"Tell him to go boil his head," Ruprecht said pleasantly.

Theo's pasty face grew paler at sacrilege.

"We'd better go up, Rupe." Trudy shrugged. "We can't afford scenes tonight."

"I'm not going," Ruprecht told her.

"But, Rupe—"

"I'm not going," he repeated. "I wouldn't listen to his crummy speech if he sent his whole bodyguard after me."

She flared up. "So you can't face it. Magda and Rudolph—"

Ruprecht sounded tough now. "If you don't stop that drivel, I'll break every bone in your—"

"I'm going." She turned on Johnnie. "Come on, you. You're supposed to be guarding Magda, not reading books."

"She didn't need me. She had two other guys." He licked his fingers, piled up his china and let the book thump to the floor.

"She'll need you now," Ruprecht supplied gently. "Now that Trudy has her knife whetted."

Trudy marched to the door, chin up. She pushed Theo out ahead of her, snapped, "Come on," to Johnnie and continued her march without looking back.

Johnnie carried his dishes after her. He didn't make the door. Ruprecht asked persuasively, "How about a little drink before you go?"

Johnnie turned around. Ruprecht held out one of the bottles of champagne. "I always carry a spare for emergencies like this. You don't really want to hear that baby Führer make a pep talk, do you? Kick that door shut and set down the crockery. We'll have one little drink. And if there's not enough here for one little drink, we'll buzz for more."

Johnnie kicked the door shut. He exchanged the dishes for the bottle. Ruprecht said, "The cork's been sprung. Do you need a glass or are you a man?"

Johnnie tipped up the bottle. He'd never tasted champagne before. He smacked his lips.

"Have a seat," Ruprecht invited. He lounged in one corner of the couch. Johnnie took the other. "How's about a little toast? Damn all women. I don't like women."

"I kinda do," Johnnie admitted.

"What for?"

"We-l-l—"

"But that's all," Rupe closed that avenue. "I say damn their golden hides." He drank. Johnnie drank.

Ruprecht said, "Particularly damn Trudy." He raised the bottle.

"I don't know," Johnnie dissented. "She's a pretty cute little mouse."

Rupe drank. "She needs beating." He held up the bottle again. "With a club. How do you stand on damning Magda?"

"We-l-l—" Johnnie thought seriously about that. "She's—she's—"

"She's a slut. Trudy's right about that. We'll damn Magda too."

Johnnie drank. "Is she really going to marry that lug?"

"Sirrah, you speak of my brother! She is if she can. Wouldn't surprise me any if she had a J. P. in the crowd just to make it legal, but quick." Ruprecht eyed him. "Just what were you doing in here?"

"Honestly, I was reading."

"Who sent you?"

"Nobody sent me. I came down here to find out about Rudamia and Trudamia and that Luxembourg. I never heard of them before."

Ruprecht's eyes widened. "For God's sake where did you come from?"

"I'm from Texas," Johnnie bridled. "And I still never heard of Rudamia and—"

Ruprecht murmured, "I should say in rebuttal that I have never heard of Texas. Unfortunately that wouldn't be true. For two years I have heard nothing else but." He clapped his hands. " 'Deep in the Heart of Texas'." He raised his voice in song. " 'Got too much of Texas in my ha-ir.' " He eyed Johnnie carefully.

"And how did you get mixed up with this den of thieves? Who are you?"

Johnnie took another swig. It was a relief to have someone to talk with at last, someone who wouldn't shut you up every time you opened your mouth. "It just happened."

"Spill it."

"I was taking a subway ride. And Pudgey—Herr Dorp—was on the same subway. And I just happened to follow him." He might as well give out with the whole works. "See, he was talking German to old Gimlet-face, the one you call Ottomkopf, and I didn't think it was patriotic for him to be talking German, not in these times."

Ruprecht looked kind of funny. "Otto doesn't speak English well. It makes it difficult."

Johnnie bristled, "I'm in the Army, see? I'm Private First Class John Brown from Texas stationed at Fort Dix in New Jersey. I didn't like that guy talking German. I was going to tell him." He relaxed. "Only he went in his house before I could, so I followed him."

"How did you get in?"

"The squirt—that guy called Theo—he let me in."

Rupe's eyes squinted. "Go on."

"Well, that's when it began to happen. I was waiting to see Herr Dorp, and Trudy came in, and I fell in the paste, and she rushed me upstairs and put me in Magda's room."

"I trust you protected your honor," Ruprecht peered down the mouth of his bottle.

Johnnie blushed a little. "Magda didn't even see me. You know. She just bossed me around, made me put

54

on this monkey suit—" He broke off, demanded, "Are these S's?" He jabbed the silver snakes on his collar. "Because I've heard of the S. S.'s."

Ruprecht sighed. "They're an imitation."

"What do you mean imitation?"

"Skip it. It's a uniform, sort of private army."

"That goon's?"

"If by goon you are referring to my unadmired brother, Johnnie, you're in the groove. Continue."

He wasn't sure yet. Even imitations wouldn't be good. But he continued, "That's all there is to it. Only I wanted to find out about those countries so I decided to look them up." Intelligent, just like Bill.

"Save your eyes," Ruprecht admonished. "I can tell you all there is to know about Rudamia and Trudamia. Rudamia is coal and iron, Trudamia is oil and mica. Divided we fall. But if Rudo and Magda get together, we aren't divided any more."

"You mean," Johnnie began bug-eyed, "like in history? They get married for state reasons?"

"You don't think she's marrying him for his manly virtues, do you?"

Johnnie took a long drink. "What about Luxembourg?"

"Well, most people have heard of Lux. Even if they haven't heard of Rudamia and Trudamia. They're all down in the same neighborhood. Only Ru and Tru aren't as big as Lux. When the Nazis rolled in—"

"You mean—"

"Don't you read the papers? But then it wasn't in the headlines. There weren't any battles. The Nazis just took us over."

"How did you get away?"

"I wasn't there." Ruprecht held the bottle upside down. Nothing came out. "I've been at Yale the last five years. Nice place, Yale. Much nicer than Rudamia. Before that, I was at Exeter."

"I'm Texas A. and M. Or I was before the war." Johnnie got back on the beam. "Did the Nazis take Magda's country too? How did she escape?"

"She wasn't there either. She's been at Miss Featherley's for years. That's where they send girls with figures instead of minds. Trudy's been at Bennington. That's for girls with figgers and minds both."

"And Rudolph?"

"Rudo had no yen for higher learning. He was at Biarritz when the shooting began. He took straight off for Alex, just in case. Smart lad, Rudo. Only trouble with him, he waited too long to get to the States. Only made it to Mexico."

"He likes Mexico," Johnnie supplied.

"Why didn't he stay there if he likes it so well? The family has a big rancho in Mexico, belonged to an ancestor. Why go back to Rudamia? But he wants to play king."

"That goon is really a king?"

Ruprecht took his tongue out of the bottle. "Empty. Absolutely empty. Not even an aroma. We'll have to go for reinforcements. Unless you'd like to wait here while I get them."

Johnnie consulted his watch. It was ten o'clock now. "I better not. I got a date with a couple of soldiers downtown. I can't be too late. They want to go to the Stage Door Canteen. I'd better go find Magda."

"Lay off Magda," Ruprecht warned. He gathered up the empties; Johnnie took the crockery. "Trudy's bad enough but Magda—she's poison. If you really want a girl, I've got a list that will lay you against the ropes."

Johnnie shook his head. "I just want to ask her something. After that I'll tell off Herr Dorp. Then I'll be on my way." He remembered his manners. "I've enjoyed the party very much, Mr. Ruprecht. Especially the éclairs and the champagne."

"Call me Rupe. And don't thank me. Thank Ferenz."

They weaved to the marble stairs, climbed fairly steadily. The ballroom was noisier than ever, climaxed around Rudolph and Magda. Rudolph was still talking. His brother said, "Sure you won't join me in another bottle? We could split one."

"Haven't time. Thanks just the same." He'd had enough. He wasn't tight, just pleasant, but he was warm. He'd enjoy getting outdoors.

Ruprecht laid his hand on his shoulder. "If I were you I wouldn't mention to anyone in these parts just who you really are. They might not like it." He wobbled pleasantly toward the bar.

Johnnie sidled back to the supper table. He ate a handful of salted nuts and a big ripe olive. He wasn't going to get near Magda soon, not in this mob scene. She was standing over near the music, on Rudolph's arm, bored stiff behind her painted smile. Ottomkopf, Janssen, Dorp and Theo were grouped around. Ferenz beamed like a goat-fed cobra. Trudy was evidently too small to show. Johnnie grabbed another handful of nuts and a couple of mints. No use standing up for the rest of the oration. He couldn't make out what the goon was saying as it was. He retired gracefully to his favorite couch. More than ever he regretted the absence of the platinum babe. He was in the mood for a blonde about now. He'd give Rudo ten more minutes. If he didn't shut up by then, he, Johnnie, would make a dive through the crowd and interrupt. He had to find out the address of his uniform.

Rudolph's voice squeaked on "Rudamia!" A burst of applause drowned him out. Must be about over. Just then Trudy came out the door. She was moving fast until she spied Johnnie. She didn't slow down then but she changed her course. She was in front of him before he could budge. "Why are you out here?"

"Just resting. I got tired standing up."

She gazed at him with an eye like Aunt Clotilda in her bad moments. "What did you do with Rupe?"

"He's gone for more champagne."

"He's had enough champagne. And so have you." She darted a quick one over her shoulder. No one was there. Her voice dropped. "Here. Take this. Don't give it to anyone but me and don't tell anyone you have it."

She'd pulled 'this' out of her gold evening bag. It was an envelope, done up with blobs of red sealing wax. It was too heavy for its size. Something besides paper in it. The jewels?

She pushed it into his hand. "Take it. Put it in your pocket, your inside pocket, stupid! Quick."

He made it quick. He was almost scared sober she was so jumpy. If anyone had come out of the door they couldn't have seen what he was doing. She was shielding him. He got it tucked inside.

She fixed her eyes on him. "Remember. Don't tell anyone, not anyone, that I gave you anything."

"Sure nuff," he nodded.

"If you do—" It was funny but he hadn't ever noticed before that her eyes weren't pure blue. Around the pupils were flecks as green as Magda's. "If you do," she repeated, and her voice was colder than the marble bench, "I don't think you'll live very long."

Three

FOR A MOMENT, but only for a moment, Johnnie observed Trudy through pinwheels. He wasn't that drunk. He had heard what she said. She was still standing there making sure he took it in. And he was right, her eyes weren't any softer than marble.

His voice gulped back into his throat. "I won't forget," he assured her quickly. All the pleasant glow had evaporated. The only warm place about him was his inner coat pocket. That was too hot.

She seemed satisfied. She looked human when she asked sharply, "Just what were you doing in the library?"

"Reading. Trying to read. I wanted to find out about those countries. Then I was interrupted. But Rupe told me about them. Magda's queen of this Trudamia—"

"Indeed she is not!" Trudy flashed. "My mother's queen of Trudamia. And I'll be queen some day. Trudamia is a matriarchy. Magda comes from a very minor branch of the family, a sixth cousin. Her father was a commoner."

Even if she had just scared him out of a year's growth, she really was cute as a bug. And she was a blonde. Johnnie took her hand. "Sit down and tell me about it," he urged. He began to feel warm again. "You don't want to hear any more of that guff, do you?" He sort of half-pulled her down beside him. She wasn't exactly reluctant. Maybe her feet hurt too. "If Magda isn't queen why is she going to marry Rudolph?"

"You don't think I want to marry him, do you?" She was indignant. "It's a perfect solution. Gets rid of Magda and Rudo both—if it comes off."

"He actually is a king?"

"He will be. If he gets back in time after the war. Of course the people would rather have Ruprecht but Rudolph is nine months older so he gets to reign. Uncle Ruffeni—their father—died this year."

"The Nazis?" he asked somberly.

"The Nazis had nothing to do with it," she retorted promptly. "He had apoplexy because some fool in Nairobi watered his cognac. That was Uncle Ruffeni. Personally I think Rupe's a bastard."

"He is not," Johnnie contradicted. "He's a good Joe."

"I don't mean a bastard that way. I mean the other way. He couldn't be Uncle Ruff's son."

He wished she'd stop talking so much. He felt like working up to a little cuddling. He moved a little closer. "You know who you remind me of?"

"Sonja Henie," she snapped. "If all the men I've reminded of Sonja Henie were laid end to end I'd drive a tank over them with pleasure." She sighed. "But he is too."

Johnnie sighed with her. "Is what?"

"A bastard that way too." She gave him a gimlet glare. "Who kissed whom?"

"Who kissed whom?"

"Rupe and Magda. Who kissed whom?"

"I wasn't watching them. Maybe it was mutual." Her mouth turned down at the corners. He recollected. "But she'd made the date and she was doing the preliminary footwork."

That was better. Suddenly Trudy reared back against his arm. "Just how did you get in on this anyway?"

"Listen, babe," he took her hand firmly, "I like that. You're the one got me in on it. You shoved me in her room and she made me put on this fancy costume. And you ask me what I'm doing here!" He remembered again what he had to do. "Listen, I got a date downtown. I'm late now. The guys aren't going to like it. I don't want to break up the party but I've got to get back and change my clothes."

"What guys?"

"Bill and Hank. My sidekicks, compadres, see? They're waiting for me at the Astor. If you'll just give me that address—"

"First you have to help me get Rudo away from here."

"*I* do!"

"Yes, you do. We must get him back to Dorp's before it's too late."

"Too late for what?"

She was holding his hand now. "Don't you **see** it isn't

61

safe for him to be running around this way. It isn't even safe to be here at Lessering's. Any minute—"

They'd been talking so hard neither one had noticed the balcony filling up. The speech was over. Not until the shadow of Ferenz loomed above them did they look up. The big guy was actually twittering. "Trudy, isn't it divine? I can't conceive of such good fortune. The announcement of Rudolph's betrothal made here, in my home." He squinted at Johnnie. "And who is your handsome friend, dear?"

"One of Dorp's men." Trudy stood up. "Come on, Johnnie. Let's us be the last to congratulate the hapless bride. See you later, Furry."

She dragged Johnnie by the hand. He muttered, "Why do you keep saying I'm one of Dorp's men?"

Her voice was clear if quiet. "How long would you last if I told the truth?"

That made a second warning. He took it. "Who is that Furry?"

"Ferenz Lessering. He's giving the party."

"He's really one of the Lesserings?"

"Munition Lesserings? Yes. You get it?"

Johnnie shook his dumb head.

"That's why Rupe can live here. Rupe's not a queer. And that's why Ferenz has been putting up the money for Otto and Dorp. The more little wars the merrier. Keeps the wheels of industry rolling."

He still didn't get it.

"You don't think the Rudamians will put up with Rudolph long without having a revolution, do you? But we must get him out of here. It wouldn't be cricket to let him be assassinated before he was ever crowned."

"You think there's danger of that here?" His eyes popped.

"This house is full of Rudamians and anti-Rudamians. The only place in New York where we know he'll be safe is at Dorp's. We must take him back there."

"How?"

The music was playing a fairly decent swing. "Might as well dance across," Johnnie said. He grabbed her before she could refuse. She could trundle all right. "How?" he repeated.

"I don't know," she confessed.

He didn't bother his head about it now. Not dancing with this little honey. He didn't even think of Bill and Hank waiting outside the Astor. He didn't bother to think until somebody rammed a fist in his back.

"You cannot do that," Dorp stormed.

"Can't do what?" Johnnie had his own fist ready.

"You cannot dance with Her Highness."

"Who says I can't?"

"Wait." Trudy stopped dancing. "I asked him to dance me over to Rudolph, Dorp. We want to get Rudo out of here. Johnnie's going to help."

"How?" Dorp shrugged.

"I could throw him over my shoulder." Johnnie was practical. "He couldn't weigh more than a Garand."

"He could bite," Trudy warned. "Have you talked to him, Dorp?"

"He would not even listen. He is having a good time. Cock of the walk. Royal Highness this, Royal Highness that. He must not miss the plane."

"That doesn't go till morning," Johnnie reminded.

"But there is much business to attend to."

"And if he gets on the Clipper drunk, he'll talk too much," Trudy said. "We've simply got to think of something."

They all thought. Johnnie suggested, "Why couldn't I take him with me to the Astor?"

"No," Trudy said.

"You aren't supposed to think," Dorp told him. "We do the thinking."

"You better think fast if you want my help," Johnnie began.

"Quiet!" Trudy commanded. She thought some more.

"I can think better when I'm dancing," Johnnie grinned. "How's about it?"

"Quiet!" Dorp commanded.

Johnnie didn't wander away. He walked off. Now was the time for action. He walked right across the ballroom to Magda. She didn't appear to be having a very good time. Everyone was crowding up to the goon. No one even noticed she was a gorgeous number.

Johnnie announced, "I'm back."

She turned, startled. When she saw who it was her eyes greened. "Where have you been?"

"Dancing. You want to dance?" He held open his arms. Either she'd been away from Trudamia too long to remember the rules or it was that commoner father. Or maybe if a fellow opened his arms she knew only one way to move. She closed in. He danced her out on the floor. The Highness didn't notice. Trudy could dance but with Magda under your chin you didn't care what it was she called dancing.

Johnnie said, "I wish we were somewhere good. This band stinks. Why don't we get out of here?"

She flung those long black lashes up at him. "I wish we could. But Rudolph—"

"We could take him along."

Her eyes narrowed and her mouth curved. "Then what would we do with him?"

Johnnie swallowed hard. He held on. This wasn't what he'd bargained for. This was worse than a bottle of champagne. "Anything you say, honey," he murmured to her cape jasmine hair. "But anything."

She pushed him away without any warning. "Who are you?"

He was getting tired of playing invisible man. He didn't get a chance to answer.

Her eyes burned. "You can't dance with me."

"What's the matter, don't you like it?"

For just a second she half-smiled. "Some other time." Then she was back to being queen again. "Of all the impudence. Royalty does not dance with commoners."

He said, "Listen. It's none of my business but I think you ought to gather up Rudo and get him out of here."

Her "Why?" was sharp. Her eyes slitted around the room.

"Trudy didn't like that scene a bit she barged into. You and Rupe on the griddle. If you don't get Rudo away where you can have him alone, there might be some sabotage. You aren't married to him yet."

She dug her fingers into his arm. "What did she say?"

"She doesn't think you're good enough for Rudolph. Your old man—"

She was furious. He lifted her claws off his sleeve. "That little—that little prig trying to wench my game. Just because her father was a Dallas millionaire."

"Did you say Dallas?" Johnnie cried joyfully.

"I said Dallas."

"Then he was a commoner, too!"

"No, he wasn't. He was a prince. But he went to work in Texas—oil. No better than a commoner." She set her teeth. "Trudy wants Ruprecht but she won't get him. He wouldn't give a phony nickel for her."

"You can't have both the boys," he told her.

She tossed her head. "Tell Theo to get the cars ready. We're leaving."

"Rudolph too?"

"Rudolph too."

"How?"

"Never mind how. Do as you're told." She didn't float; she plunged toward her fiancé.

Johnnie returned to the thinkers, still thinking in the same old spot. "Tell Theo to get the cars," he ordered. "We're all leaving."

The two of them raised incredulous round eyes. "How?" they Indianed.

Johnnie spoke haughtily. "Wouldn't you like to know?" He didn't remain with them. He sidled back to the buffet, stuffed his pocket with salted nuts, lifted a last chocolate éclair and finished it in three bites. He was well pleased with himself. All this how business. All you had to do was use your head. Nothing to it.

It didn't do any good to try to get in the car with Trudy. The setup was as it had been earlier. Even to the cordon trudging off on foot. Johnnie had the same uncomfortable jump seat.

Rudolph was doing the talking just as he had on

the trip over but he was more jittery now. "How do you know there were F. B. I. agents at Ferenz' party, Magda? How do you know they were there? How do you know they aren't following us?"

Magda had known how to use her head too. Nothing to it. Johnnie grinned and lit a smoke. He blew it toward Janssen, sitting there stiff as a ramrod.

Magda said, "Never mind how I know it. It's my business to know. And they aren't following. We didn't parade out of the house, did we? We melted away quietly. Even if they were following, the boys have orders to give them the slip."

"How do you know they won't come to Dorp's house when they see I'm missing? How do you know they won't follow us there?"

She didn't say, "Stupid," but her voice implied it. "Dorp is a respectable professor of languages at Columbia University. No one is going to break into his house. And if they did, what would they find? A respectable house. That downstairs would fool anyone. It's hideous."

"Suppose they came upstairs? Suppose they—"

Janssen snarled, "Make him stop it, Magda. He's getting me nervous. I can't afford to be caught by the F. B. I. It's all right for the rest of you but I can't afford it. You know I was enrolled in the party before I got away. I couldn't help it but I was. They'd find it out and shoot me. How *do* you know we're safe, Magda?"

Magda said wearily, "For God's sake, Louie, don't I have enough on my hands without you going to pieces? If you and Rudo can't take my word for it, I'll get out of this car right now and you can stew in your own juices. Now shut up both of you. You make me excruciatingly ill."

"But Magda," Rudolph whimpered.

"Light me one of your cigarettes, Johnnie," Magda interrupted. "Or are your hands shaky?"

"I'm not afraid of man nor beast," Johnnie drawled. "Or the F. B. I." He almost swallowed that one with a gulp. If the F. B. I. really were on the trail, how was Private Johnnie Brown going to explain wearing this monkey suit instead of his G. I. uniform? He passed the cigarette to her. There wasn't any F. B. I. That was her contribution to spiriting Rudolph back to Dorp's.

Rudolph stammered, "I wish I were back in Mexico."

Magda didn't say, "So do I." She merely began to hum, "Get Out of Town."

The car pulled up in the quiet side street, stopped short.

Rudolph quavered, "Where are we? What is it?"

"Dorp's," Magda said.

"Where is Dorp? Where's Trudy?"

"They're already here. We came roundabout purposely. I told you that."

Rudolph backed into the corner. "How do you know they're—"

She drew a breath. "I say they're here. They're here. Now get out."

"Before I beat your brain in," Johnnie murmured to himself. He helped her to the street. She rushed ahead up the stairs. He stuck with her. The rest pattered after them. It wasn't Theo who opened the door; it was Trudy, sparkling white in the dim hallway.

"Hiya, Babe," Johnnie greeted her.

"Go right on up." Her mouth was grim. "I'm waiting for the squad to get here."

Johnnie followed Magda. Dorp was pacing up and down, his short arms behind his back, his fat face red as the velvet throne. Theo was standing in the corner chewing his fingernails. Dorp waited only until the five, trailed by a wheezing Ottomkopf, were inside. Then he exploded. "Theo has lost the papers!"

Ottomkopf fell back. "It cannot be!" He was hoarse. His eyes were like broken glass now.

"Do any of you have them?"

Johnnie shook his head along with the rest of them. Rudolph asked, "What papers?"

"Your passports. Your identifications."

"But I have them," Rudolph began.

"Idiot!" Dorp raged. "You have the ones to take you from this country to Europe. You do not yet have the ones to take you from Switzerland to Rudamia. The true ones." His eyes opened hopefully. "Or do you?"

"I have never seen them and you know it." He flounced to the throne chair and extracted from his pocket the long cigarette holder. "You know very well I haven't seen them. You told me you'd give them to me when I boarded the Clipper."

"Theo has lost them," Dorp repeated with menace. "I keep them on me until we go to the party. Then I think it is not wise I carry them there. They do not look so well in the full dress suit. Perhaps Ferenz will grow snoopy. He is so afraid we do something outside the law, something at which we get caught. He would not like doctored papers such as Rudolph must use to enter his country. So the last thing in the car I pass them to Theo. He has big military pockets to keep them safe. And Ferenz does not like Theo." His little eyes narrowed. "Because Theo does not like Ferenz." He shrugged. "Does he put them into the inner pocket as anyone with the brains of a peahen would do?"

Johnnie had the papers! He realized it suddenly. This didn't seem exactly the time to disclose that fact. Besides Trudy had been insistent he keep mum. More than insistent. She'd threatened him. He kept his mouth shut. Despite everything he liked Trudy a lot better than this passel of thieves. He didn't like Dorp at all.

"No!" roared Dorp. He slapped his fat thigh and winced. "He puts them in his coat pocket where when he leans over to make the bow they fall out."

"They couldn't have fallen out," Theo blubbered. "I told you, Herr Dorp. The envelope went way deep."

"Someone picked his pocket," Magda said. "That's obvious. In the crush while Rudolph was speaking. Who was near you?"

"I don't know." There were tears in Theo's eyes. One hung from the tip of his nose. "I didn't notice. I was listening like Herr Dorp told me to." He wailed, "I didn't want to carry the papers. I didn't want to be responsible."

"Enough," Ottomkopf commanded. "You will turn in your uniform, be confined to quarters." He looked about the room. The rear guard hadn't caught up yet. The only uniforms were Janssen attending Rudolph, and Johnnie following Magda. "Who will escort him?"

"I know the way," Theo sniffled. "I'll go." He turned at the door. "If you'd only told me the inside pocket, Herr Dorp. But you said pocket."

"Go. Go on!" Dorp waggled five thick fingers. Theo went.

"It's Ferenz." Magda scowled. "Of course it's Ferenz in back of it."

"But why?" Dorp shook his head. "He is paying good money for Rudolph to go. And he knows nothing of the false papers."

"When you've known Ferenz as long as we have, Herr Dorp, you won't ask why. You'll know that everything he does is to make trouble and sell some more of his nasty bombs and stuff."

Rudolph almost fell off the throne. "You think Ferenz doesn't want me to return to Rudamia? Because I won't go if that's the way he feels. After all I owe him a hundred and fifty thousand rudls. Besides he might be planning another revolution."

"He might be," Magda admitted. She sat on the throne steps and put her chin in her hand. She surveyed the ruby lovingly. "But in that case why wouldn't he let you go ahead? A revolution's no good without a king to dethrone. And he promised me I could be queen. He even got the betrothal ring out of hock."

"There are no revolutions in the new Rudamia," Dorp swelled up.

"There can be," Ottomkopf countered.

Dorp stuck out his chin. "Saupreussen!"

Ottomkopf turned the colors of roquefort. He couldn't get his tongue to work.

Magda said, "I wish you'd be quiet. I'm trying to think how we can get Ferenz over here now." She stood up. "I can't think in these clothes. I'm going to get comfortable. Don't start any more name-calling until I return. Save that for Furry."

Rudolph said, "I want to take a bath."

"Now?" Magda turned on him violently.

"I don't know when I've had a bath," he said dreamily. "I've heard so much about American hot water. You and Trudy and Rupe were always bragging about it. I want a bath now."

"Don't drown," Magda said with set teeth.

"Janssen will show you your room," Dorp said.

Magda added, "Get back before Ferenz arrives." She sailed out. Johnnie was in her wake. She didn't turn around until she was on the floor above, outside her door. "You can't come in. I'm going to change."

"I want to change too," he said. "I don't like these clothes."

"Why not? On you it looks good."

"I want my own uniform."

"A uniform's a uniform." She slammed the door behind them.

It was not. This snake thing wasn't anywhere near as good as old G.I. He didn't mention that. Not with two warnings not to talk too much. He was looking around. His suit wasn't here yet. He said, "I guess Trudy hasn't brought my things up yet."

"For heaven's sake why should she bring them to my room?" Magda demanded.

"Well, she put me in here to dress, didn't she?"

"God knows why." Magda had the white skirts half

72

over her head before he could yell, "Wait a minute!"

"If you're still squeamish," she retorted, "get out."

He started for the door.

"No, don't." It was a command. "I want to talk. I've got to talk."

He did the next best thing. He turned his back and sat down. He said sadly, "My uniform ought to be back by now."

"Keep quiet about your uniform," said Magda through a mouthful of dress. "How can I go about getting Ferenz over here? That's the trouble. He's so full of good manners he won't walk out on his party. And he didn't want to see Rudolph in the first place. He made the best of it, that's Ferenz, but he didn't like it." Her mouth was empty now. "Well, why don't you say something."

"I want my suit," Johnnie said.

"Your suit! You worry about a suit when I have this to contend with!" She was quiet for a spell and then she said, "You can turn around now, Johnnie. I'm decent. But think, how can I make Ferenz come? It's got to be good."

She was more than decent. She was a thriller. Yellow slacks, yellow sweater, black velvet coat and sandals. She was rolling a yellow chiffon handkerchief to tie around her black hair.

Johnnie had a brainstorm. "Business," he stated.

"What business?"

"Tell him it's business. Tell him there's a new war started, lots of business for him."

She whirled from the dressing table. "Darling!" She plastered a kiss on his yellow cowlick.

"Don't *do* that!" Johnnie murmured, not loud.

She dipped some more magnolia perfume, touched her chin. "But of course. That will bring him. Why didn't I think of it before? I'll tell him there's a revolution broken out in Rudamia. We just heard it over short wave. We need his help. He'll have to come then. Rudamia's royal family owes him too much money to let the country go Bolshie."

There was a white phone by her bed. She stretched herself full length on the fluffy white coverlet. Johnnie gazed at the rug. She was made for sweaters, or maybe she wasn't. He lit a cigarette.

She said, "It's most important that I speak to Mr. Lessering, Shanks. Call him at once." Her voice stroked the space between the bed and Johnnie. "Whoever you are, you're a lamb and a love. I don't know why Dorp didn't bring you around sooner. Why don't you come over here?" She patted the edge of the bed. There wasn't room for a toothpick on that side of it.

Johnnie felt his ears turn scarlet. He just shook his head.

"You're a darling. Hello—hello—Ferenz, Magda." Her voice became throaty, conspiratorial. "We've just heard the most awful news. Rudamia has revolted against the Nazis. Bolshies. You'll have to come over at once. I know but this is important. Don't you understand? We must decide what to do about Rudolph. We can't send him into that and we don't dare keep him here. No! Don't tell Ruprecht—he'd just upset Rudolph." She nodded her gorgeous head, smiled at Johnnie. "Yes, Furry. You do understand? You will come? Angel! Hurry!" She replaced the phone and stretched her arms above her head. She laughed. She reminded Johnnie of a leopard he'd seen once at the circus. She looked at Johnnie between those foot long eyelashes. "You don't want to come over here?"

Johnnie breathed deeply. "Not now." He breathed some more. "I really haven't time. I have a date downtown I'm late for." He'd get back to Trudy, find out what she'd done with the uniform, and he'd skip out fast. Before anything more happened. He wasn't used to babes like this one.

"You'll have to break it." She leaned on an elbow. "But I had better get downstairs and tell them Ferenz is coming. We'll have to plan an attack. The dirty bum. Snatching those papers." She patted the yellow chiffon back in place. "He isn't easy to work on. Come along, Johnnie."

He waited until she had the door open before he moved. He didn't want to get any nearer than that to her. His neck was damp enough. She didn't speak again until she reached the door of the throne room. "Go down and tell Trudy he's coming so she'll wait for him." She patted his cheek. "You're sweet as well as smart, Johnnie."

He ducked down the flight to first but fast. This was the break. Tell Trudy. Trade her the papers for his uniform and beat it.

She was sitting on the straight chair, a deserted white cherub. He said, "Everything's under control, baby. Ferenz is coming."

She jumped up. "What for?"

"I forgot. You don't know." He glanced upstairs. No one in sight. He lowered his voice. "Anyone hear us?"

She motioned him down on the steps, sat beside him. "They think Ferenz took the papers." He patted his left upper pocket. "So Magda's called him up and told him there's a revolution on in Rudamia and he'd better get over and decide what to do with Rudo. Only there isn't any revolution. We sort of thought it up together," he admitted modestly. He talked fast under his breath. "When he gets here they're going to try to get the papers. Only he hasn't them." He stuck his hand toward his pocket. "Where's my uniform? I got to be going now so you'd better take these and—"

"Going?" Her blue eyes were rubber balls.

"Sure. I told you. Or I've told everybody else. I got a date."

"You can't go now. It's too late."

"It is late," he admitted. "But Bill and Hank kind of expect me not to turn up on time. They'll keep looking. Where's my suit?"

"I mean you don't dare go. They'd nab you if you left now." Her hand touched him. "Listen, Johnnie, you don't think they're going to let anyone leave here, not until the papers turn up, do you?"

He stuck out his chin. "Then I'll give them the damn papers."

"You can't do that!" She put her face up to his. "How are you going to explain where you got them?"

"You gave them to me."

"Do you think they'd believe you? A—a strange soldier—? When I said that it was all a big lie?"

He leaned just a little bit closer and he kissed her. Like that. She jerked back. He said, "You're cute, baby. Even if you are a stinker."

"I'm no baby. I'm no stinker either. Johnnie," she softened up again, "the cleaner hasn't sent your suit yet so you'll have to stick around just a little longer. It'll be here by the time we get Rudolph on his way, I'm sure. You can stay that long."

"I cannot," he denied. "Why can't I go around to the cleaner's myself?"

Her face fell. "Johnnie!" She whispered it. "With the F. B. I. watching the house?"

"They're not," he moaned.

She nodded. "Come here." He followed her on tip-toe to the front door. She pulled aside the shirred curtain covering the glass. He peered over her head where she pointed. "See that man across there in the shadows? There—in the door of that house."

He squinted. He could see flickering shadows. It might be a man.

"He's been there all evening. He's either F. B. I. or he's one of the Young Terrorists."

"What are they?" he asked hoarsely.

"They're an organization avowed to end the Ruffeni reign in Rudamia. They'd as soon kill you as look at you." Her eyes held fright. She scuttled back to her chair. "You don't dare appear out in that uniform."

"But—" He followed her to the steps, sank down. "But they let us go out earlier."

"Safety in numbers," she nodded sagely. "Anyone who goes out alone is simply walking straight up the gallows." She added more cheerfully, "Whether that man's a Terroristi or an F. B. I."

He was stuck. Plenty stuck. He sighed down to his toes. It was late. Getting on to eleven. Bill and Hank might not be looking for him. They'd probably picked up a couple of cute chicks themselves by now. He hadn't told Dorp off, either. And he would like to know what it was all about. Mom and Dad and the kids would pass right out from curiosity when he wrote them about tonight if he didn't know any more than he knew now. He decided. "I guess I'll stick around for a while."

"Good." She brightened. "I'll probably need your help to get Rudolph out of here."

"Just till my suit gets back," he warned her. He tipped his head with curiosity. "Tell me something. Why did you snatch those papers?"

"I want to examine them."

"Let's." His hand dived but she pulled it away from his pocket fast.

"Not here!" She whispered, "I'll arrange it so we can slip out after Ferenz gets here. You keep them until then. They're safer on you than me. No one would suspect you of having them. A Rudamian patriot."

"Is that what I'm supposed to be?" he asked.

"That's what you are tonight," she told him with emphasis. "And don't forget it. Not till I can take over the papers. You'd better go back up now and see what's going on. If there's any funny business, let me know."

It was all funny business as far as he was concerned. He didn't say so; he just grinned, "A'right, honey."

She ducked this time.

He drawled, "I need target practice. Be seeing you, sugar. And don't forget, let me know as soon as my suit gets here." He went on up the stairs. He didn't knock at the throne room, just moseyed in. Nobody paid any attention to him. The S. S. boys were all back at attention, standing around. Dorp and Ottomkopf and Magda were in a huddle by the throne. She was sitting on it; Rudolph wasn't around. Johnnie picked an inconspicuous far corner chair and sat down to rest. The guard shielded him from the three big shots and he could hear plenty. Dorp didn't know how to talk below a shout.

"I still cannot believe it was Ferenz," he was yelling. "Think of the money he has put up! Why would he steal the papers which cost so much to procure?"

Magda said, "But Ruprecht wouldn't want them. I tell you he doesn't want to be king. All he wants is to stay in New York and drink and rhumba."

"In the German Army this could not have happened," Ottomkopf stated nastily. "It is this untrained guard you have."

"You try to do better," Dorp shouted. "In Germany I could do better but here—how can I train with what I have to train—"

Johnnie didn't like this talk of Germany. He knew now he wasn't going to leave until he'd told off Dorp and Ottomkopf in full.

"If you two don't get together," Magda stated, "at least until Rudolph's out of the way, I'm going to walk out right now. You just try to manage him without me!"

"Now, Magda," Dorp began.

Ottomkopf puffed, "That is not fair, Magda. You have give your word you would help us if we—"

The door opened. The guard stiffened. Trudy announced sweetly, "Here he is." Ferenz bounded into the room.

He was wringing his plump pink hands. "Magda, but this is unbearable, dear. When everything was so perfect—"

"Sit down, Ferenz." She pointed to a chair ringed with the guards. "I'll tell you all about it. Get Rudolph, will you, Trudy?"

"Where is he?"

"He's taking a bath," Magda gritted.

Trudy departed. Unobtrusively a part of the guard reformed until they blocked the doorway.

"Now tell me, dear," Ferenz breathed. "What did you hear? It is execrable that right now—why, I had the word of every leader!"

Magda rested her head against the chair. "I lied to you, Ferenz. There's no revolution."

The big man jumped up. He squealed, "No revolution! Why then—"

"Sit down, dear," she repeated softly. "We want to talk to you."

She wasn't depending on glamorous persuasion. She held her gun pointed directly at Ferenz' stomach.

2.

Magda continued, "Captain Janssen's men are here to see that you do sit down, Ferenz. That's better."

Ferenz fell back in the chair. He was shaking like a jitterbug. He stuttered, "Mmmmmmagda! I don't understand this."

She tucked the gun back into her jacket pocket. "You will. Tonight at your house, someone stole the papers that Rudolph must have to cross the Rudamian border. We want to know why."

"Mmmmmagda!"

Her eyes glittered. "We want to know why."

"But Magda, I know nothing about any papers—"

Rudolph came pushing through the crowd. Trudy wasn't with him. He had on a purple satin bathrobe with a gold crown on the pocket, purple velvet bedroom slippers with gold heels. His legs were skinny. "Ferenz, why did you take my papers?" he demanded.

"I don't know anything about it." Ferenz rolled his eyes. "Why should I take the papers? I want Rudolph to be king. I'm paying for it that he should be king. Why should I take his papers?"

"Stop beating around the bush," Magda said sweetly. "They were stolen in your house."

"I know nothing of it," he swore. "I can't believe it. Have you looked?"

"They are gone," Dorp scowled. "Gone before we leave your home."

"It wasn't I," said Ferenz. He raised a sudden forefinger. "Ruprecht!"

"That's who it was," Rudolph agreed. "That's exactly who I thought it was. He's jealous."

"Folderol!" Magda snapped. "Rupe doesn't want to be king any more than Johnnie does." She glanced around for him. He slid down into the chair and hoped the guy six paces in front of him wouldn't budge. "You'll have to come across better than that, Ferenz. If you didn't do it, who did? Who did you hire to do it? Who was there?"

"No one there would do it! I tell you that. We've been planning ever since you left. After the war we'll charter two clippers and fly across for the coronation.

Oh, we had the sweetest plans, really we did. Everyone wants you to be king, Rudolph."

"The servants?" Dorp piped hopefully.

"They are all utterly loyal," Ferenz declared with a noble leer. "To me and to Rudamia," he added.

Magda sighed. "We've had enough of this runaround. Either you turn over the papers, Ferenz, or—" She eyed the guard meaningly. "Or you go upstairs."

Ferenz turned green. "Oh no, Magda. You wouldn't dare do that. Not to me."

"I'd dare anything," she told him, "to be queen."

Dorp and Ottomkopf both nodded. Some of the guards shifted uneasily.

"Magda, dear, I don't have them," he wept. "You must believe me. I'll do anything you can think of to get Rudo away in the morning. Money is no object to me now. All I have spent on Rudo means nothing. Gladly will I spend more. Anything. But I can't give you the papers. I've never even seen them."

Johnnie was getting tired of this. Obviously the big guy was telling the truth. Sure he was. The papers were in Johnnie's own pocket. He wished Trudy would come back. He wished she'd plan that sneak and turn over the damn papers. He was getting sleepy. And he wanted a drink of water.

Ottomkopf said, "Have you any suggestions, Duchess Magda?"

"Couldn't we buy another set?" Ferenz asked eagerly.

Dorp shook a sad head. "We have worked for three whole weeks getting those papers made so they will pass any inspection." He looked wary. "I mean so they will not be discovered what they are before he reaches Switzerland. Could I do that again before tomorrow morning? The answer is no."

Rudolph dropped ash to the red velvet rug. "Somebody must have them. And I don't think it's Ferenz."

Ferenz smirked weakly.

"But this has gone far enough. Whoever has them must give them up. If they don't—" He tapped his head. "I shall now get dressed. If they do not turn up before I come back I shall—" He tapped harder. "I know what I'll do. I'll go straight to Washington to our own government-in-exile. I shall tell them everything."

"Not everything!" cried Ferenz, Ottomkopf, Dorp and Magda.

"Everything!" Rudolph said snippily. "I shall leave to them my safe return to Rudamia—or Mexico."

"We could send you back to Mexico tonight," Ferenz cried eagerly. "That's safe enough."

Rudolph weakened but he pulled himself up again. "Not until after I have talked with our government-in-exile. Unless of course the papers are returned before I finish dressing." The guard made a wary path for him. He banged the door.

Dorp drooped. "He cannot talk. Not that he knows much."

"He knows too much," Ferenz squealed. "Where will I be if he goes to Washington? The F. B. I. will listen in on all he has to say. Every one of us—"

Johnnie perked up again. There was something more than squirrel stuff here. They were all afraid of the F. B. I. They weren't on the up and up. And it wasn't jewels.

"I will be ruined," Ferenz whispered starkly.

Ottomkopf spoke slowly. "He must not talk."

The guards shifted weight again in the silence. Johnnie could see even better now.

Dorp said, "If only we can find these papers in time." He turned purple. "That dumkopf. That Theo."

"You should not have trusted something that important out of your hands," Ottomkopf gloated. "You Herrenvolk are all alike, afraid you will be caught at your dirty work. A Prussian would—"

"Seupreussen!" Dorp screamed again. "Don't you tell me nothing. How do I know you did not take them yourself just to get me in trouble?"

Magda ordered, "Stop it. Rudolph's upstairs now scurrying into his clothes and you—all you can do is call names." She closed her eyes. "I think I'd better go talk with Rudo."

"Yes," Ottomkopf nodded.

"That is good," Dorp beamed. "A little more time we get."

Ferenz leaped to his feet. His finger pointed dramatically. His voice was hoarse. "Who is that hiding in the corner?"

He was pointing directly at Johnnie. The guard had shifted once too often. They widened out now.

"I'm not hiding," Johnnie said. "I'm resting."

Magda was impatient. "That's one of Dorp's men. The one who attended me tonight."

Dorp peered. "He is not one of my men. I do not know him. I never have seen him until you bring him downstairs with you tonight. I think that you—"

Magda turned on him fast. "He is too one of yours. Trudy brought him to my room tonight. She told me—"

Johnnie stepped up to her. "If you'd have listened to me at the beginning, Magda, I'd have told you I wasn't one of his men. Instead you kept telling me to keep quiet every time I opened my mouth." He glared at Dorp. "But you're wrong on one thing, Pudgey. You did too see me before I came here tonight. I stood right beside you on the subway. I came here purposely to see you. I wanted to tell you we're in a war. A war against Germany. And when we—that's Hank and Bill and me and the rest of us—get through with those Nazis, there isn't going to be anybody talking German. Not unless he wants a kick in the teeth. I came here to tell you that it isn't patriotic for you to be riding around on the subway talking German like you were tonight. But after some of the other things I've heard in your house I guess you don't care whether it's patriotic or not. All I hope is that the goon does go to Washington. I think the F. B. I. should know about you folks."

He turned on his heel, started to the door.

"Where are you going?" Ferenz howled.

"To the Astor. That's where I'm going. Not that it's any of your business, Bub." He turned again. G. I. suit or no G. I. suit, he was getting out of here. He whirled back just in time. Horse sense. Two of the guards were almost on him.

He kicked one in the belly, wrenched the other's arm out of its socket. This was what he'd been waiting for. This was what he'd been learning in camp, to fight dirty against Nazis. He threw the fellow across the room right into Dorp's fat face. They crashed together.

Two more guards were at him. He flailed, got one in the Adam's apple and one below the belt. The other members of the unit held back. He didn't blame them. He swaggered, "Come on. I'll take you all together."

"You needn't," Magda said. He looked at her quick. She had the blunt-nosed automatic pointed right at him now. "I won't shoot to kill if you make one move, Johnnie. I'll shoot where it will hurt the most without hanging murder on me. Maybe you learned about that in camp." She ordered Janssen, "Take him upstairs. Tie him up. Tight."

Janssen started forward with soldierly stride. Johnnie made a horrible face at him. Janssen stood still. "Do you think we should?" he asked. He was listening to the groans of the men on the floor, watching others rubbing their anatomies.

Magda's lip curled. "What do you want to do? Let him walk out and bring back the F. B. I.?"

It had never occurred to Johnnie to do any such thing. Even if he was in uniform it wouldn't appeal to him. They'd just think he was a drunk soldier on a pass and he'd land in the brig. They wouldn't believe what happened tonight. Dorp and his buddies would all be safely on the Clipper or in Mexico or under Lessering's important name while he, Johnnie, languished in the clink.

Magda continued with disgust, "I'll go up with you, Louie. I'm not afraid of him." Her green eyes smiled unpleasantly across at Johnnie. "He's afraid of me but I'm not afraid of him."

Janssen barked an order and two untouched guardsmen came gingerly forward. More gingerly they took Johnnie's arms. He released his arms. "I'm not aiming

86

to get shot," he told Magda, "but I don't want no panty-waists helping me to walk. Which way?"

"Upstairs," she said.

The two guards walked behind him. Janssen was behind them. Magda and the gun brought up the rear. Johnnie might have made a run for it but he preferred to keep whole. He was perfectly certain she'd be able to shoot crooked as well as straight, and the openwork banisters wouldn't be any protection. On the third floor she marched him to the door at the back. Janssen opened it. The room was small, evidently Theo's from the large framed photograph of the squirt looking chinlessly soulful at his crossed knee and a cigarette. Johnnie had always meant to have his picture taken that way for the kid sister but he'd never had the nerve. He was glad of it now.

Janssen stepped ahead to open the closet door. At the back of the closet he slid away the wall. Johnnie whistled. He'd never actually believed that anyone had trick houses like that. New York City was all that it was cracked up to be. Beyond the opening was another staircase. Janssen went ahead to the hidden fourth floor. The corridor was dark until Janssen pulled on a small overhead light. There were only closed doors visible and there wasn't any velvet carpeting on the floor.

Magda waited while Janssen turned the knob on the door at the front. He pulled another overhead light. It was a little dinky room. Four old kitchen chairs, a battered table with a burned-down candle in a broken candle holder, nothing else in it. Johnnie's mouth set. Must be the torture chamber. Where nobody could possibly hear you, nobody could see you. The only window was a small triangular attic one at the front. It wasn't big enough to crawl out of even if you felt like gymnastics.

Magda ordered, "Tie him up."

The guards looked at Janssen. Janssen looked at the guards. All turned hesitantly to Magda.

She frowned. "You're not still afraid, are you? I have the gun. Tie him up."

"What with?" Janssen asked.

While Magda was gathering fury Johnnie plopped down on one of the chairs. The guards jumped at the sound. He explained, "My feet hurt."

Magda shouted, "With what! Idiots! Cretins!" She gathered more breath. "Nuts! Go get a rope. Get wire. Get anything. Go. I'll watch him. Go. GO!"

They went fast. They clattered down the steps. Magda sighed. "Can you imagine such fools?" Without turning she pushed a chair far across the room from Johnnie, sat down, laid the gun on her crossed knee. "If you move I'll shoot you."

"I won't move. Can I smoke?"

"If there's a trick to it, I'll shoot you."

"There's no trick." He lit a cigarette. There wasn't. He just wanted a smoke, that was all.

"I suppose you think I should shoot you now?"

"Oh no!" he reassured her.

"Dorp would. Or Otto. It would be safer. But I've never killed anyone yet."

Johnnie swallowed hard. He hoped she wouldn't start tonight. She seemed to be considering it.

"That's one reason. More important, if anything

should happen I don't want a murder pinned on me."

"I should hope not," Johnnie agreed weakly.

"There's always the problem of getting rid of the body and we haven't time for that now. Although it isn't much of a problem."

He gulped. "Maybe it wouldn't be if I were just John Brown back home in Texas but I'm not."

Her gun jumped into her hand. "Just who are you, Johnnie Brown from Texas? Where did Trudy find you?" Her lip curled. "And why?"

He'd been warned to keep quiet but he was too mad now to worry about that. And too scared. Well, not exactly scared but he didn't feel very safe at the moment. "She didn't find me. I came here to see Herr Dorp. For a good reason. And I better get out of here safe too. I'm important. I'm Private John Brown. I live in Uncle Sam's house. If anything happens to me—" He swallowed the lump. "If anything should happen to me, he'd find me."

"Not if I got rid of you, Johnnie," she said with certainty.

"That's what you think. He'd have a million M.P.'s out looking for me. They'd find me. Don't you think they wouldn't. They'd find me whatever you did and they'd find you, too."

She laughed. "You're really quite stuff, Johnnie. I wouldn't want to shoot you. It's too bad you don't like me better. We might have had some fun. Don't you like me at all?"

His tongue was thick. "You're mighty pretty."

She laughed lazily. "Is that the best you can do?" Her eyes narrowed. "I suppose you prefer blondes."

He knew better than to irritate her. She was twirling the gun. "Oh no, ma'am," he vowed. "I like blondes and brunettes. And redheads."

He remembered with a pang that redhead back on the campus. He'd meant to write to her. If he ever got out of this whole, he would write to her. He'd ask her for a picture. She was funny-looking with a turned up nose and freckles. He never wanted another sultry beauty pinned above his bed.

"Perhaps we might get together if you're that versatile."

"I'd like to," he cried. He lied in his teeth. Well maybe not that bad but at the moment there was nothing he wanted less than playing games with any girl.

"Some other time," she smiled.

Johnnie took the bull by the horns. "Just what are you going to do with me? You can't leave me tied up here forever."

"I could if I wished," she said coolly. "But it might make the house smell." She smiled wider. "Only a few days, Johnnie."

"Few days!" He leaped up.

"Sit down," she suggested, with the gun pointing smack at his middle.

He flopped. This was the worst news. "I can't be gone that long. My pass is only good till Sunday morning. I have to be back in camp by four A.M."

"I'm afraid you'll be late, Johnnie."

"But I can't be late. I have to be there. Don't you understand? I'm in the Army. What will my top sergeant say?" What wouldn't he say.

"I'm so sorry," she said lightly.

He glowered at her. "I'm sorry I didn't throw that guy at you instead of at Dorp."

"I thought you might be."

He had to do something about this and quick. But that gun wasn't fooling. Neither was Magda. He tried to reason with her. "Why do I have to stay here that long?"

"We must get Rudolph away."

"But you're going to do that tonight."

"Not without the papers."

Well, he could give her the papers. He could hand her the damn papers right this minute. The same two reasons held him back. One was Trudy's nervousness about their contents. And she had a gun too. The other was what might happen to him if suddenly he did admit to having them. That wasn't a pretty picture.

"You needn't worry, Johnnie," she said. "Of course you will have to explain to your top sergeant why you're late for Sunday breakfast but nothing is going to happen to you."

"No, nothing," he groaned.

"You'll be perfectly safe. It's necessary that we tie you up so that you won't gum the works but you won't be hurt. Just as soon as possible you'll turn up safe somewhere. By that time it won't do you any good to bring back the Marines. We'll all be gone."

And he'd be trying to explain what looked like A.W.O.L. He'd be better off if she did shoot him. He stuck out his jaw. "I'd bring the Army if I came back not any Marines. But I wouldn't come back here for a million dollars. Or for the biggest farm in Texas. You couldn't pay me enough to come back here." He shook his head. "You couldn't let me go by **tomorrow night** if I promised to say nothing?"

"I'm afraid not." She turned on the reappearing guards. "What did you do, knit it?"

They held what looked like a clothesline. "We had to wait for Trudy," Janssen explained.

"And where was Trudy?" Magda was suspicious.

"Nobody knew," Janssen said. "But I found her."

Magda clutched the gun more firmly. "Where was she?"

"With His Highness."

"Snip!"

"Well, she saw you with Ruprecht," Johnnie reminded her.

She swung to the guards. "What are you waiting for? Tie him up!"

Johnnie didn't make any false moves, not with that steel eyeball poking at him. He did offer one weak protest as his hands were lashed behind his back to the chair. "How'm I going to smoke with my hands tied? I won't be able to smoke."

"Won't that be too bad?" She inspected the job unsmiling, nodded her head. "Janssen, we'll go back down now. Post a man on this door." She turned mocking eyes on Johnnie. "Hawg-tied, as you say in Texas, don't you?" She bent down, kissed his mouth. "You are cute, you know."

She didn't look back at the color of his ears. Only four lonely walls knew they sizzled.

3.

Hawg-tied. That was Johnnie. Those saps in the black suits didn't have any muscles but they knew how to lash a man fast. If he were smart like Bill or tough like Hank he wouldn't be in this stew. He'd be thinking right now of a way to get loose. He was thinking only he couldn't think of a thing. What could any guy do tied to a chair in an attic bedroom? Yelling wouldn't do any good. Or would it?

He opened his mouth and bellered, "Help! Murder! Police!"

It sounded pretty silly to be yelling all by yourself. It didn't even sound loud. All that happened was that skimpy guy outside the door stuck his head in, took a look, and yapped, "You be quiet." The guy had a rifle now. He pointed it ahead of him awkwardly when he barged in. He went right out again, banging the door after him.

That settled making a row. No one could possibly hear, no one but that dumb rookie outside. Even if sounds carried below, that bunch wouldn't investigate.

Dick Tracy would have a piece of glass or a nail file hidden between his fingers to saw the rope. Johnnie didn't. Superman would swell out his muscles and break the ropes. Johnnie tried that one. Well, he'd never claimed to be Superman. Jungle Jim would have a faithful friend crawling through the window to release him. Johnnie didn't have a friend within thousands of miles except Bill and Hank and they were too busy cutting a rug at the Canteen to worry about their poor partner.

What would Bill do? Bill would never have shoved into a mess like this in the first place. He'd have reasoned that old Pudgey Dorp was a German professor not a Nazi. Only Johnnie wasn't too sure yet about that. Dorp could be both. He acted like a Nazi. Plenty of those downstairs acted like Nazis. And those uniforms looked just like Nazi uniforms in the movies.

What would Hank have done? He'd have socked Dorp right there on the subway and he'd have told everybody in earshot why. He'd have a medal on his chest by now, not yards of clothesline.

The door clicked. Johnnie scowled at it. His eyes opened. Rudolph, the goon. All dressed up in a pearl gray suit with pin stripes, a lavender spotted tie, lavender hanky sticking out of his pocket. All sweet and perfumed. Probably not perfume, just the grease oiling down his black hair.

If this panty-waist had come up to make with the Nazi tricks, he, Johnnie, would hit him with chair, rope and all. But Rudolph hadn't. His mouth was drooping open. "What does this mean?" he was complaining. "What are you doing?" He acted as if Johnnie had staged this only to annoy.

"I'm waiting for the expressman," Johnnie replied.

"I don't understand."

"Cut yourself a piece of brain. You don't think I tied myself up in a package, do you?"

"Who did?"

"The Damnazis," Johnnie stated with emphasis.

He hadn't expected Rudolph to take it this way. The goon's face went pearlier than his suit. He cringed. "Nazis! Are they here?"

"What do you think? The place is full of those Nazi soldiers."

"Oh," cried Rudolph relieved. "Those aren't Nazis. They're the Rudamian guard. Maybe some of them had to join the S.S. when the Nazis marched in but they got away. They don't belong any more. No one in Rudamia wants Hitler. They don't like him. They're going to throw him out."

"They and who else? They couldn't even throw me out, and I don't live on top a mountain."

Rudolph said, "At first you frightened me. I thought perhaps I had been tricked by the Nazis. I will not return and be one of their puppet rulers. They approached me time and again in Egypt and I just told them I will not be a puppet ruler. I shall return only as a rightful king of Rudamia to rule as I choose. No other way." He finished his speech and was curious again. "But I still don't see why you're tied up here in this dreadful little room."

"I tell you it was the Nazis." Johnnie was using the old bean now. "You don't think they're here because they've fooled you. What do you know about Dorp?"

"Magda said—"

"Magda wants you to be king so she can be queen. She doesn't want to wait till the war is over. She doesn't care who she plays with so long as she gets to be queen."

The prince was getting queasy again.

"Anyhow what does she know about Dorp? She's a woman," Johnnie said smoothly. "Maybe he's fooled her too. But he doesn't fool me. Talking German and Munich this, Munich that." He demanded suddenly, "Who comes from Munich?"

"I won't be made a fool of." Rudolph shuddered. "But I'm afraid of Nazis. They're brutes."

"Now you're jiving," Johnnie complimented. "If you'll just untie me, we'll get out of here."

"Get out?" Rudolph piped.

"Yeah. Get out. But quick." He coaxed, "You want to get out, don't you? You don't want to be a Nazi puppet, you said so."

"I want to be King of Rudamia," said Rudolph simply.

"You won't get to be King of Rudamia if the Nazis tie you up too and leave you here to starve to death."

"Starve?" Rudolph faltered in falsetto.

"Starve," said Johnnie grimly. "Now will you untie me?"

The goon still hesitated. "I don't know whether I ought to. Whoever tied you up might not like it."

"Well, you'd better," Johnnie menaced. "You aren't going to like it a bit when the police come and find my body up here and arrest all of you for murder. You'll never get to be King of Rudamia then."

"Police?" Rudolph's face was as spotted as his tie.

"Sure, the police. Listen, I don't know how they do it in Rudamia but over here if somebody gets killed the police come and they haul everybody down to head-quarters"—he drew on his moving picture experience —"and they keep giving them the third degree with rubber hoses until they get a confession and then—" He decided he'd better cut before Rudolph fell flat on his face. He concluded, "So you'd better untie me so I can get both of us out of here before somebody gets killed."

Rudolph wiped his lavender face with his lavender handkerchief. "How will you do it?"

"Leave that to me." Johnnie spoke with assurance. Not one hundred percent but Rudolph couldn't know. "It'll be a pipe to get the gun from that phony guard. Why did you come up here anyway?"

"I heard Magda's voice, in that back room downstairs. By the time I finished dressing, she wasn't there. I thought maybe she'd been coming up here. There wouldn't be any other reason for her to be in that room."

"You discovered the secret door?"

"I knew about it. Ottomkopf told me before I left Mexico." He tittered. "How the guard comes up here without anyone knowing, to drill and hold meetings. And how if anyone questions them on the street, they say they are actors, dressed for a performance."

"Drill in this cracker box?" Johnnie scorned. "No wonder they are undersized. Start with the hands, Rudolph. Get them loose and I can do the ankles."

Rudolph began fumbling in back of the chair. "There's a room beyond this, a big one. This little one is for committee meetings." He was panting like an Airedale pup. "I can't budge these knots."

Johnnie's heart zoomed down into his toes. He wiggled them. Then he perked. "Listen, in my right hand pocket you'll find a knife. Stick your hand in. I'll try to lift up a bit. My pants pocket. And no hooking the folding dough there." He strained at the ropes until Rudolph could edge in a hand. "Any trouble getting past that guard?"

"Certainly not. He saluted and I came in."

"What did he say?"

"Nothing. I am his commander. The Rudamian guard has never been loyal to that dreadful man. They wish reinstatement of their rightful rulers." He drew out the Scout knife. "Is this it?"

"Open the big blade and start sawing. I'm pleased to hear you're the commandant, brother. If Nosey peeks in tell him to mind his own business. Saw away and mind the arteries."

"I still don't see what good this is going to do."

"You'll see," Johnnie told him. "I'm tough. I've been trained. We'll get Stupid's gun—he doesn't even know how to handle it—then we'll march right out of here and if anyone gets in our way they better duck." There was the rear to be considered on the march. "You don't by any chance have a gun, do you?"

"Oh my no!" Rudolph exclaimed. "Otto made me carry one on the trip but I'm rid of it. I loathe firearms of any sort."

"We'll risk it just the same." Maybe he could back down the stairs with Rudo as a shield. No one here would potshot the future King of Rudamia. "Once we're out we'll grab a car and I'll drive you to the airport. I'll see you get on the Clipper. How did they get you into this mess in the first place?"

"It wasn't a mess. It was wonderful." Rudolph stopped sawing for the moment to heave a sigh. "Rudamia wanted me to return. Most of Rudamia. Only there's a man—he used to be in charge of the royal stables but he didn't like Father. You see, Father used to sneak down to Kraken's house while he was currying the horses and steal his brandy. That was when Grand-mother put Father on brandy rations."

"Keep sawing. Where's your Grandmother now?"

"She's in Lisbon. She's running a bar there. Father died of apoplexy last year."

"So I heard." Johnnie nodded. His hands were free. "Now give me the knife. You got a mother?"

"She divorced Father when I was quite young. She lives in Hollywood. She's married to a big producer there."

Johnnie cut the chest and thigh bonds. "Why don't you go home to Mother?"

"I'd rather be king," Rudolph stated. He was light-ing one of his fancy cased cigarettes. He dusted a chair with his lavender handkerchief, perched on the edge of it. "That's what I was telling you. The people want me, most of them, but Kraken wants to be president of Rudamia. He tells them lies about me. So unless I can get in fast after Hitler is run out, Kraken will force himself on the people."

"Tough," Johnnie murmured. He stepped free. Deliberately he took up the rope and began cutting it into tiny chunks.

"Why are you doing that?"

"For fun," he retorted. Nobody would tie him up again with this line. Maybe they would have to knit the next.

"Colonel Ottomkopf—he prefers Herr Ottomkopf in these times—is a Prussian baron who has long been the military adviser of our kingdom. He first got wind of Rudamia's planned revolt against Hitler and then he met Dorp who corroborated it. Otto thought I should return, wait in Switzerland until the time was ripe. I had to get out of Mexico anyway. The Nazis had found out I was there. They were watching me. I never saw them but Otto did. They wanted to take me back to be a puppet king, then you see they could hold on to the country for themselves even with Hitler gone. I won't be a puppet king."

"Don't blame you," Johnnie grunted.

"Ferenz fixed it up that I could travel over the border. He's very clever. I pretended I worked for one of his companies in Mexico. The Nazis were after me then, right on my trail. But Otto put me safely on the plane. The trouble is I have to be careful here too until I can get on the Clipper. If the United States government knew that Rudolph of Rudamia was in town, they would intern me."

"Why?"

"I don't know why." He was petulant. "I've written them about it time and again. They let Ruprecht stay here but they refuse to let me come into the country."

"Rupe was in before Rudamia went Nazi, wasn't he?"

"What difference does that make? I'm more important than he is. But no. They refuse entrance to me—me! Even my government-in-exile hasn't helped me. Surely the American government cannot believe I am in sympathy with those loathsome Nazis. Peasants! Not a one of them has a pedigree."

"Bust mah britches," Johnnie murmured. "And now if you'll light that candle for me."

"What for?"

"I want to read a letter." Johnnie moved to the table.

"Is there time? Hadn't we better get away first?"

"Won't take a minute," Johnnie said.

Rudolph's hand wobbled with the match. Johnnie took the letter from his pocket. He heated the pen knife and lifted seal upon seal. There were a lot of papers. He examined them.

"Who's it from?" Rudolph asked.

Johnnie moved to the other side of the table. "My girl." There was nothing wrong with these as far as he could see. Just Rudo's real passports and pedigrees. But the weight of the letter had been too heavy. He removed from one fold the thin brown cylinder. And he stared at it.

"Why did she send you a cigar?" Rudolph wanted to know.

His voice was shaky. "Cause I keep running out of cigarettes." Here he'd been whamming around with the Rudamian boys and this in his pocket. No wonder Dorp had passed it to Theo at the party. He wouldn't have wanted to take any chance of trouble with this on him. Theo didn't count. Theo was expendable. But what hit Johnnie right between the eyebrows was that neither did Rudolph count. He wasn't supposed to reach Rudamia. He was going to carry this thing with him on the Clipper. It was the kind of thing that spies packed in boxes so ships would explode in mid-ocean. Johnnie'd learned about them in bomb strategy.

He let out his breath. It couldn't be harmful until morning. It wasn't to be handed to Rudo until then. Rudo might investigate the contents if he had it sooner. Dorp certainly didn't intend to blow himself up. Johnnie carefully put the cigar in his right hand coat pocket. He heated the knife again, pressed down each seal until it stuck. "We'd better get going, Rudo. I mean going places. You aren't safe here." He blew out the candle, replaced the letter in his inner pocket.

Rudolph paled. "You really mean you think—"

"I know, son." Johnnie nodded grimly. "After this war you can throw a party for me in Rudamia. The guy who saved you from sudden death. Now you step out and speak to the guard and don't worry about what I do. Don't mention my name." He spat on his hands.

Rudolph went first. "Good night," he quavered.

Johnnie caught the guard on the first heel click. A right behind the ear, swing him, a left to the jaw. He grabbed the rifle as the fellow crumpled.

Rudolph squealed, "Why did you do that?"

"Remember, I'm saving you from sudden death," Johnnie vowed. He grimaced at the prone guard. "If we have any luck he won't wake up until we're safe outside. Now listen, Rudo, we'll try strategy. If that doesn't work we go into Commando stuff. You walk ahead. I follow with the shoulder arms—like this. If anyone says, 'What cha doing?' you say, 'One side, Joe.' But if any of the big guys turn up we change around, me in front, fix bayonets, and then we rush the can. Get it?"

"Not very well," Rudolph admitted. "Half of what you say has never been intelligible to me. But I shall try to follow you."

Johnnie patted his shoulder. "That's the old one-two."

They met no one in the descent to Theo's room. The corridor without was dim, silent. Rudolph pulled

Johnnie's sleeve. "I'll have to stop in my room for a minute."

"What for?"

"To get my suitcase."

Johnnie was apprehensive. "Do you have to?"

"Oh, my yes!" Rudolph whispered. "There's seven thousand dollars in it. I can't leave that behind."

Johnnie could understand that even if he didn't like the waiting, now they'd come this far. Maybe that guard wasn't out as far as he'd looked. He agreed reluctantly, "All right, we'll stop."

"You wait outside," Rudolph warned. "I won't be a minute. Keep watch."

He opened a cautious door at the left, here at the back of the house. Johnnie was glad of its location. He didn't want to be near Magda's room, right front. No telling what she might think up if she caught them sneaking out. Rudolph had closed the door after him. Johnnie stood in the semi-darkness listening to the thump of his heart. It didn't sound good. He hoped Rudo would step on it. Thirty seconds seemed long. And then, unmistakably, he heard footsteps below. He ducked inside the room fast.

Rudolph jumped from the closet, holding a topcoat and a soft gray hat. He shrilled softly, "What is it?"

"I don't know," Johnnie said. He held the door, listened. "Somebody's coming up or going down. Either way it isn't good." He pressed his ear to the crack. "I don't think we'd better try it that way," he decided. He had an idea.

He pushed past Rudolph toward the windows. Before he got quite there, he stopped. The way the bed stuck out had hidden this thing. A guy lying flat on his face. A big hole burned in the back of a pepper and salt topcoat.

Only a gun made a hole like that.

Four

THE MAN'S black Homburg lay half under his head. A suitcase was on its side resting under the pepper and salt arm. The man didn't move. Johnnie bent down, lifted the head by the black hair. It was Theo. Johnnie dropped the head and wiped his hand on his pants leg. He kept wiping it. He felt a little sick.

He'd never heard a throat rattling before. Rudolph stood behind him. "Dead?" he whispered.

Johnnie nodded. He was thinking about this. It was all his fault the squirt was killed. That made a fellow feel terrible. If he hadn't held on to the papers, Theo wouldn't be lying here dead.

"Why is he in my room?"

Johnnie said heavily, "I suppose he was coming in to tell you he was still loyal even if he had made a mess of things."

Rudolph said, "No." He said it one word at a time as if he couldn't make his tongue move. "No. He was running away. My room's on the fire escape. It isn't really my room. It's Trudy's."

That was the first time Johnnie noticed the room. It

was a girl's room, all clean delft blue and white and a big framed photograph of Ruprecht on the dressing table. It was signed: For Baby Mine from the Wolf.

Theo had been running away. There was his suitcase, a battered brown one, to prove it. Rudolph's grip was a smart affair, striped, over by the bureau. Theo was running away because everyone was down on him. And it was Johnnie's fault that everyone was down on him. Theo was scared of what Dorp would do. Dorp had done it. Johnnie's muscles knotted. He'd beat the hell out of Dorp before he left here.

"Come on. We must go quickly." Rudolph put on his hat backward, struggled with his topcoat and grip. "This is terrible, terrible."

"We're not going," Johnnie said.

"Not going!"

"We've got to call the police."

"The police!" Rudolph screamed. "We can't call the police."

"We got to," Johnnie repeated. "When you find a body, you have to call the police."

"But if the police come they won't let me leave. They won't let me be King of Rudamia. You told me so." Rudolph's chin wiggled. "I don't want to stay here. Not after this dreadful, terrible thing has happened. In my room, too."

"That's another reason we can't go. Suppose we skip out. What happens? Whoever rubbed out Theo gives the police our identification tags and we're picked up. If we run away nobody's going to believe we didn't do it, or at least that you didn't. The room is full of your fingerprints."

"Of course it is. How silly. But I didn't do anything wrong."

Johnnie hadn't even considered that. Rudolph could have before he came upstairs. No. He was too dumb.

"Why would I do it?"

"Because he lost your passports."

"I didn't."

"No cop would believe that if we hightailed." Johnnie looked hard at him. "That's one reason why we're not skipping. The other is that somebody's got to pay out for this. We're going downstairs and tell that gang we found Theo. And we'll see who isn't surprised. Then we'll call the police. We'll see who doesn't want us to call the police."

Rudolph took off his hat. "I don't like this."

Johnnie shouldered the rifle sadly. "Who does? Come on, Prince. Nobody's going to hurt you. Not now."

Rudolph followed timidly. There weren't any guards at the throne-room door. Johnnie opened it. "You first," he told His Highness.

Rudolph walked in. Johnnie followed with fixed bayonets.

Magda cried, "Rudo!" She wasn't expecting him, that was a cinch. She had her yellow slacks hanging over the arm of the throne chair, her black velvet shoulders resting on the other arm. She looked comfortable. She looked alluring. The allured was Janssen sitting at the foot of the throne. He picked up the two highball glasses before he jumped to attention, before she rolled to her feet. "Rudo, where have you been?" She looked beyond him and scowled. "You're supposed to be tied up."

"I untied him." Rudolph gazed balefully at Janssen.

"Why?"

"Because I wanted to." He kept his eye on Janssen. "Where are the others?"

"They're going over Ferenz' guest list name by name. Trudy's phoning everyone to see if anyone picked up those papers by mistake."

"Ruprecht stole them," Rudolph said.

"She's trying to find Ruprecht too. She's calling all the night spots but she hasn't caught up with him yet. Where have you been, Rudo? We've looked everywhere."

"You didn't look in my boudoir," Johnnie stated harshly. "Have her go get the others in here, Rudolph."

"Janssen will get them," Rudolph ordered.

Johnnie added, "Ask them to come in here and don't tell them who or why. Get it?"

Magda patted the throne. "Come sit down, darling."

"I'll stay here," Rudolph told her frigidly. He took a stance closer to Johnnie.

Janssen had walked only to the end of the room. He knocked on a door there. Someone out of sight slid it open. Janssen said, "Will you come in please? All of you. By request."

Dorp emerged first, Ottomkopf, Ferenz, last Trudy. She'd changed her white skirts too. She had on pink slacks and a pink sweater and a pink ribbon around her yellow hair. She looked about the age of the kid sister. Only Sis hadn't filled out yet.

Ferenz burbled, "Rudolph!" Dorp echoed it. Trudy didn't say anything. Ottomkopf said something in German. Trudy was looking at Johnnie and his gun.

"Where have you been, dear?" Ferenz asked. "We

searched for you. We thought maybe you'd left." Dorp and Ottomkopf kept staring.

Johnnie got it then. Rudolph had threatened to go to Washington. Theo and Rudolph looked pretty much alike. In a dark room—Rudolph's room—a man with a suitcase was Rudolph. Rudolph had been killed. Only it turned out to be Theo. Which one had fired the gun? Everyone of them had been surprised when Rudolph showed up. He wasn't expected to show up. There was even a goat for the killer. A dumb private from Texas, the stranger.

Johnnie nudged the gray pinstripe ribs. "Tell 'em."

"What?" Magda cried. "Tell us what."

Rudolph shivered. "We found Theo. He's dead. In my room."

Johnnie watched faces. They all managed to look amazed. Ottomkopf demanded, "Who is Theo?"

"He was my lieutenant," Dorp said. "The dumb one who lost the papers."

"Oh," said Otto, almost pleased.

Trudy's little voice cut through. "In your room, Rudo?"

"Yes. It's disgraceful. Actually the room is yours but I was using it. And I don't like such things."

Johnnie said, "Somebody shot him in the back. Some dope. Anybody with the sense of ducks would know he was the only one who might remember something about those papers."

"He should not have been killed," Dorp agreed.

"I'll say not." Johnnie shifted the rifle. "Well, where's the 'phone? I'm going to call the police."

"The police?" They all said it and they all looked faintly surprised and more than faintly worried.

"Sure, the police. You have to call the police when there's a murder."

"Maybe it was an accident," Ferenz began.

"You can't accidentally shoot yourself in the back. Anyhow you have to call the police for an accidental death too. I know. My Uncle Tom was Sheriff of our county once."

That didn't go over at all. Dorp eyed the others. "It is true. The police must be notified." He didn't mean it.

"After Rudolph leaves," Ferenz smiled.

"Certainly. After Rudolph leaves." Dorp rubbed his fat head. "We would not jeopardize the plans by calling now. It is not long to wait."

Johnnie shook his head. "You can't do that. You have to call the police right away."

"Young man, will you kindly mind your own business?" Ferenz sputtered. "You've caused enough trouble tonight as it is. Besides I thought you were tied up."

"I didn't like it," Johnnie swaggered. "I don't wonder you're scared of the police. You must be the worst hoarder in New York."

"I am not a hoarder." Ferenz' face turned bright red. "Every bit of food in my home tonight was produced on my own farm."

Ottomkopf accented, "Why do you waste words with this speciman, Mr. Lessering?"

Ferenz raised elephantine shoulders. "He taunted me."

"And you're afraid of the police." Johnnie jumped on Herr Ottomkopf with both feet. "Because you're a German and they'd turn you over to the F. B. I."

Ottomkopf fixed him with two glazed eyes. "I am a Rudamian."

"You're a Prussian!" Rudolph interjected. He was ignored.

"I am here by permission thanks to Ferenz Lessering."

"I wouldn't want that to be investigated," Ferenz said.

"And you," Johnnie swung on Dorp. "You're nothing but a scrub of a Nazi. You killed Theo. Rudo and I know why you killed him too. You meant to kill Rudolph but you made a mistake in the dark. You wanted to kill Rudolph so he couldn't go to Washington and tell about you."

Rudolph kept gulping.

Ottomkopf demanded coldly. "Why did you dismiss the guard, Herr Dorp?"

"A lot of good they'd do. A lot of good they did before." Johnnie swelled out his chest. "Let's stop beating around the bush. I'm going to call the police right now. And soon as they get here Rudolph and I are heading for the airport. I'm going to see he gets on the Clipper safe."

"Oh no you're not," Trudy said. She said it from behind Johnnie and it wasn't her finger poked into his lower spine. "You're going to drop that shotgun right now or you're going to get plugged in the back like Theo was. One—two—"

Johnnie dropped it. It made a bang big enough to

cause all the audience to jump. Ferenz put his hands over his ears. Johnnie kicked himself. Why hadn't he kept his eye on Trudy? He ought to have known by now that the girls in this roost had more backbone than the men.

Rudolph was complaining. "You can't do this, Trudy. This man is helping me."

"Helping you?" She laughed out loud and pushed the hole deeper into Johnnie's spine. "Sure, he's helping you. Right into an internment camp. He isn't one of your Rudamian patriots. He's an American soldier. He's even got dog tags. Look under that shirt. Private John Brown, United States Army."

Rudolph raised doubtful eyes at Johnnie.

"Sure, I'm in the Army," Johnnie admitted. "But—"

"He's a government spy," Trudy said. "I've known it all evening but I didn't want to worry you. I thought I could handle him until we got you away."

Johnnie's mouth and eyes opened.

Rudolph scurried over to Magda. "And to think I almost let him take me away from here."

Johnnie had found his voice. "Rudolph, listen, of all the awful liars—"

Trudy jabbed the gun. "You're going back upstairs, soldier. Janssen, bring that rifle and come along. This time you won't get untied. Put your hands out in front of you, Johnnie. Much safer than over the head."

"Rudolph, listen," Johnnie plead.

Rudolph was drinking Janssen's and Magda's drinks, one in each hand. He shook his head.

Trudy ordered, "March."

Johnnie marched. Same old '76. Let a girl pull a gun

on him. But these girls weren't fooling. He was smart enough to know that. The men might talk but the girls acted.

He hesitated on the third floor. "Listen, Trudy—"

"March," she commanded. "Open the door, Janssen."

The fellow circled Johnnie to obey. Even if Trudy were holding a gun, Janssen was still nervous about getting in front. Johnnie waited until the man had the knob in his hand. He couldn't resist. He gave the chief guard a good hard boot in the behind.

Janssen howled, "Ow!" He jerked around.

Trudy pushed with the gun. "Stop that nonsense, Johnnie. Go on, Janssen."

Janssen, rubbing his rear, climbed on up. He was out of sight before Johnnie and Trudy entered the closet. When they reached the upper hallway, he was bending over the sniveling guard. He ducked away from Johnnie. "He hit Wallie!"

"He hit me twice!" Wallie humped on the floor, rub bing his jaw.

"What did you do to him?" Trudy demanded.

Wallie whined, "Nothing. Not a single thing."

"Why not?" She jabbed at Johnnie. "Go on in there. Janssen, you and Wallie come too. You'll have to tie him up."

The rope lay in jagged segments all over the floor. Johnnie's boot pushed at one of them cheerfully. Janssen and Wallie looked woebegone.

"What's the matter?" Trudy asked.

"He cut the clothesline!" Janssen informed her.

Johnnie grinned. "What you going to do? Splice it?"

"Sit down." Trudy pushed. "In that chair. Take your belts, boys. Strap him to it."

"My belt?" Janssen held on to its Sam Browne magnificence. Wallie gazed at his, transferred his attention to the despoiled rope, and stepped backward.

"You heard me," Trudy said. "Do as I say."

Slowly, unhappily, the two guards removed the leather. They weren't fooling when they approached Johnnie. They hated his guts. If Trudy hadn't been present they'd have jumped him and he knew it. The straps bit into his ankles, crunched his wrists.

Trudy rammed the gun into her waistline. "That ought to do it. You may rejoin His Highness."

"And you?" Janssen inquired.

She put both hands on her hips and lifted red hot and blue eyes to him. "If you're not careful, Louie Janssen, you'll lose those bars on your shoulders. Even if Magda is making a play for you. Stop trying to think. Obey orders. Get out of here before I lose my temper. I'm remaining to question the prisoner and I don't want your big ears in on it. Is that clear? Beat it. Blitz. Leave that door open and go."

Janssen and Wallie clattered. Trudy didn't move until she heard the sliding panel of the closet replaced. Then she ambled over, slammed the door. She returned to Johnnie. "Where are the papers?"

"What's the idea of tying me up?" he demanded.

"If you'd had any sense you wouldn't have tried to get loose in the first place. You're safer up here. If you can catch a little sense you'll stay tied up this time."

"You think this is fun?"

"I think it's a lot safer here than below just as I told you. If the F. B. I. agents decide to break in you'll have a much better explanation if you're tied up in the attic than if you're holding his princely hand downstairs."

Johnnie hawed. "You were seeing shadows. That F. B. I. stuff is a lot of bunk. Magda thought it up to get Rudo to leave. After I told her you were trying to snake him."

"You told her that?"

"Because you'd seen her smooching with Ruprecht."

"You told her that!" In another minute she'd pop him one.

"Well, you asked me to get Rudolph away."

"You didn't have to go that far. Letting her think I cared what she and Rupe were doing. I don't care that." She spat. "Now where are those papers?"

"If you'll loose my hands—"

"I won't and if you don't tell me where those papers are quick"—she flipped up the gun again—"you're going to have half an ear less in three seconds."

"They're where they've been. Reach in my inside pocket." He scowled. If she'd release his hands alone he'd take a particular pleasure in holding her up by the heels until she hollered Uncle. The brat.

She swished the envelope under his nose, turned it over and over. "Did you open it?"

"It's sealed, isn't it?" he glowered.

She seemed to be weighing it on her hand. Finally she ripped the seals.

He warned her, "You can't seal it up again if you do that."

"I don't intend to. When it's found, no one is going

to know who had it." She sat down at the table, read carefully through the papers, read with a puzzled scowl. "Is this all there was in it?"

" 'S all." After he'd answered her, he realized she'd stuck him with that one. But she didn't pay any attention. She was rereading the documents. "You're sure this is all? Because there's nothing wrong with these, Johnnie, not a thing."

"That's what I figured."

"You said you didn't open it."

"I've got x-ray eyes," he grinned. "How about letting loose my hands so I can smoke?"

"Hold on." She darted into the hall.

Well, there'd been no harm in asking. She had vanished. He heard doors opening, closing. And then suddenly she was there again. She had a key in her hand. She turned it in the door.

He tried not to duck when she walked over to him. He kept telling himself she was only a blonde chick. But he couldn't help the feathers blowing up and down his spine. Not when she went behind him. And then all at once his hands were free. He couldn't believe it. He looked at them, rubbed at his wrists. "That bastard buckled too tight."

"What did you expect? You kicked him. Undo your own feet."

He was wary. He didn't get this. He asked, "You won't shoot?"

She looked like a kid but her eyes were wise as hell. "Don't be an ass," she said. Her eyes were looking not into his but down into his soul. "I need your help."

2.

Trudy perched on the table and riffled the precious papers. Johnnie walked around getting the blood to circulating in his ankles.

"I don't get it, Johnnie," she admitted.

"What did you expect to find?" He stood on his toes.

"Treachery. I distinctly heard Dorp tell Theo to keep that envelope on him and tell no one. Later I heard Theo tell someone over the phone that Rudolph would never reach Europe. That's all I heard. It wasn't in the car. It was before we left the house. I didn't get a chance to pick his pocket until we were at Ferenz's. But there isn't anything here to stop Rudolph." She tapped her knuckles against her teeth. "I must reach Ruprecht."

"You haven't yet?"

"He isn't in the bars. That was a smoke screen to keep them quiet below. I know where he is."

"Call him."

"No phones. He's in one of two places. One's a little beerstube up on Columbus. Just a hole-in-the-wall. He likes it there. The other—" She bit her lip. "The other is a woman's apartment. On West End. That's where you come in."

"Me?"

"You've got to go get him."

"I got to get the police."

"I'll call them. You get Rupe."

"Listen, honey—"

"I know. But I'll take care of details. I'd do it myself only I don't dare leave. I don't know what they might think up while I was away. You'll have to do it."

116

"But honest," Johnnie argued, "I don't know a thing about where Columbus is or the West End or nothing. I've never been in New York before tonight."

"It's easy. Look. You just walk down to the end of the block and that's Columbus. Turn left. Middle of the block, right hand side. You can't miss it. Go there first. If Hans hasn't seen Rupe tonight then you walk over—"

"Wait a minute."

"All right." She repeated directions. "You have it?"

He nodded. That much was clear.

"If he isn't there, walk back over to Broadway. That's the other direction. Go downtown to a Hundred and Third Street. It isn't far. Then turn right and walk the same direction you did to Broadway, west. West End's the next street. It's an apartment house. The Dragham. The name is"—she raised her nose—"Edna Riggens." She went on very fast. "She's a dreadful person but Rupe likes her. He likes so many people. Mostly women. That's half his trouble. You will go get him, won't you?"

"Sure I'll go," Johnnie was hearty. "There's nothing I'd like better than to go." He eyed her. "But not without my own clothes."

She eyed him right back again. She was little and tough but she knew when she was beaten. Right now. "All right," she nodded. "You sit tight. I'll fetch them."

She unlocked the door, closed it after her. But she wasn't taking any chances on him. He heard the key turn in the lock. He lit a cigarette. At long last he could break out of here. He'd deliver the message to Rupe and then make tracks for Times Square. He'd probably never find Bill or Hank at this hour but that wasn't important. The main thing was to get away.

The key rattled in the lock. Trudy reentered bearing his uniform on a hanger. She said, "Pick up your shoes outside the door and lock it again."

He did. She handed over the uniform. For a hurry-up job and the shape it had been in, it looked pretty good. It didn't even smell too much of cleaning fluid. He sniffed, "How long has this been back?"

"For hours," she said airily.

"Then why in thunderation—"

"I wanted you here." Her cobra smile vanished quickly. "I had a hunch I'd need help, playing a lone hand against this field." She urged, "Well, go on. Get dressed."

"Where?"

Scorn lifted her nose. "Since when are you so particular? Go on. I've seen your underwear before tonight."

He pulled off a boot. "There's no more privacy here than at a reception center."

She didn't pay any attention to him. She was walking up and down, her hands behind her back. "You will find Rupe for me and bring him back, won't you?"

"I'll see he gets here. But I don't see any reason why I should walk back into this bear trap. I've been waiting for hours to get out of the dump."

"Because I need you." She stopped in front of him. "Don't you see it's Rupe and me against the field? And if you two don't return—"

He pushed her out of his way. "Are they Nazis?" he demanded.

"I don't know. I don't know what Dorp is. Maybe he's

a Nazi. Maybe he's of the Terrorists. He brought Rudolph here to kill him."

"I don't get it."

"If he's a Nazi and can get rid of Rudolph, they can put a puppet king on the throne. The Terroristi want a president."

"What about Ruprecht?" Under cover of the shirt, he transferred the cigar.

"He doesn't want to be king. He'll abdicate in favor of anyone. He'll do anything to keep from being king."

Johnnie took an inner squint at it. "Why didn't some of you tell Rudolph what it was all about? Why did you let him walk into this?"

"I didn't know, stupid. I didn't know until tonight that anything was wrong. Of course I didn't believe all that stuff about Rudamia wanting him but I knew he wasn't safe in Mexico with the Nazis gunning for him, and he couldn't come here. His government-in-exile told your state department they absolutely would not have Rudo in their hair. So I thought it would be fine if he could be sent as far as Switzerland. My mother's there and she would keep an eye on him. The others still don't know there's anything wrong. Magda wanted Rudo to come so she could get her claws on the crown. Otto's a royalty boy. He wants to play Metternich for twenty-five more years in Rudamia. If he's the one who puts Rudo back on t hethrone, he's set, don't you see? And Ferenz—well, I guess he has so much in the hole now that he has to keep the Ruffeni heirs in the saddle until they pay off. He's the one that found Dorp and Dorp's running the show. Rupe and me haven't had anything to say."

"You could tell them now," Johnnie suggested.

"Tell them anything!" she snorted. "Don't you understand? Dorp is Ferenz's pet. They're all so used to doing what Furry says—because of the money of course—they'd never believe me."

Johnnie turned his back to button his trousers. "But how you going to keep Dorp from killing Rudolph? If that's what he wants."

She frowned. "I'm going to stick right with him. He's waiting for Rupe to show up with the papers. Something about those papers means death for Rudo. I can't fathom it but I know it's true. Dorp's not going to make a move until he knows for sure they won't turn up. As long as he believes he can put Rudolph on the Clipper, he won't risk his fat neck."

"What do you mean he's not going to move? Theo's dead, isn't he? He wasn't killed because he was Theo. You know that. Dorp or whoever had the gun thought it was Rudo sneaking out. Bang."

"That's true," she admitted. "But that was different. It was because of the F. B. I., not Rudamia. You get Rupe for me and—"

"And what?"

"He'll snake Rudolph out of here. Then—"

"What?"

"Leave it to me." She was a chubby pink cherub but he didn't doubt her abilities.

"O. K. I'll get him." He jerked his tie under the second button.

"And you'll come back with him?"

"I don't know. But I'll fetch Rupe for you. And you'll

call the police right away? We don't want to get in any serious trouble."

"I'll call them. Don't worry about that."

"How do I get out without being caught?"

"That's easy." She walked to the far wall, shoved it open. There wasn't any door you could see, just wall, but it opened. She reclosed it. "The house next door is Dorp's too. Just in case of emergencies. He didn't tell me but I found out. No one lives there but an old lady —a cousin of Dorp's. She's in Brooklyn for the week end. You just go on through and out the front door."

"How do I get back in?"

"There's a key in the hall table drawer. Take it with you. Can you make it in the dark? Better not turn on the lights."

"I can make it." He started to the wall.

"Wait." She caught his arm. "Wait." She took a packet of safety matches from her pants pocket, lit the candle. "Turn out the light." He obeyed. She carried the candle to the front window. She kept it in front of her while she signaled some message. He couldn't get it. She said casually, "You wouldn't get out otherwise. But don't mention it to Rupe. He doesn't have to know everything."

It struck him then; he might be walking Ruprecht back into a trap. Two princelings at one fell swoop. Well—he still had a string to his bow. Good thing he'd held it out. That bomb might come in handy yet.

She pushed the wall again. "Make it quick, Johnnie. It may take you an hour but make it quick as you can. They'll want to start to the airport in plenty of time.

I'm sorry I can't let you use one of the cars but I'm afraid to risk that. You will hurry?"

"I sure will."

She turned her face up to his. Unaccountably she closed in. He didn't question it. Her arms went around his neck. His arms went around her. He kissed her. It was a kiss. And then he yelped.

"Now I know you'll come back." His dog tags dangled from fingers. The dirty little tramp, rubbing the back of his neck, cutting the plastic cord while he was otherwise engaged. She must have cut it, nobody could break one of those things.

He lunged but she had a smile and the gun aimed at him. The gun wasn't fooling any more than it had been earlier. "Run along, Johnnie, and hurry back." She closed him in behind the wall.

It would serve her right if he didn't go looking for Ruprecht. It would serve her right if she never laid eyes on him again. Only what was he going to tell the sergeant about losing the dog tags? You couldn't lose them. Not unless somebody sawed your neck in two jerking them off. And there was still the problem of the dead body. Somebody would have to call the police eventually. With him missing, who would they claim did it? Private First Class John Brown of the United States Army. That's what he got for giving his right name.

He had to go back. What's more he wanted to go back. He wanted to get a crack at those Nazi-Rudamians. Dressing him up in a Nazi uniform and parading him across town. Making him think it was a chauffeur suit. He wasn't so sure Magda wasn't in on the plan to knock off Rudolph. Not the way she'd honeyed up to

Ruprecht. He wasn't so sure Dorp had killed Theo. After all Dorp and Theo had been pretty chummy. Magda, moreover, had a pretty curious glint in her green eye when she said she'd never killed a man. Then there was Ottomkopf of the glassy glims. And Ferenz Lessering of the Lesserings, making deals with Nazis even if he did make munitions to kill Nazis.

He wasn't so sure of Trudy's wanting Ruprecht merely to get Rudolph away. If that was it, he, Johnnie, could do the job a lot quicker. How was Ruprecht going to help? He and Rudo were not aficionado. Johnnie found the key in the hall drawer. He stuck it in his pocket. He opened the front door cautiously, slipped out, closed it without sound. There were men walking down the street on this side, up the street on the other side even at this hour. There was a fellow and his girl doing some smooching on the stoop of the house across the way. No cops. No guards. No Terroristis that Trudy had dreamed up to keep him from skipping. And nobody paid any attention to him. He walked fast, his heels hitting hard on the pavement. Wasn't far to Columbus Avenue. He found Hans' place easy enough. Late as it was, the door opened. Hans was a long, tall drink of water with a scar taking up most of his right cheek. The place smelled good, like beer. It was a little joint, two booths, three red-checkered tables pushed together. The only customer was a big black cat. Johnnie clinked down a quarter. He had time for a beer. He'd take time for a beer. He needed fortifying.

Hans asked, "What kind you want?"

"Anything wet." Johnnie drank from the bottle. "Rupe been in tonight?"

"Who is that?"

"Ruprecht of Rudamia."

"That is what I think you say." Hans shook his long head. "Who send you? Kraken?"

"Never heard of him." He had but he couldn't remember who it was.

"I have not seen Ruprecht for one week," Hans said. The cat had slant green eyes just like Magda's.

Johnnie said, "His cousin wants him to come home." Trudy called Rupe's father Uncle Ruffeni; that should make them cousins.

"You know his cousin?"

Hans might be too chatty; he might be one of Dorp's stool pigeons. Johnnie said, "Sure. Just came from a date with her. She asked me to drop by and see if he was here."

"He lives at Ferenz Lessering's," Hans stated with importance.

"He isn't home." Johnnie finished the beer, took up his change. "Thanks. Which way to Broadway?"

"Right across town." Hans pointed.

Johnnie didn't walk back to Dorp's street, not with Hans maybe watching him. He went on up another block before turning crosstown. He tried not to keep looking over his shoulder but somehow he couldn't help it. The brownout was practically a blackout here uptown. He felt better when he crossed Broadway and there still wasn't anybody following him. Now down to 103d. The blocks going this way were short. He swung along getting back his confidence. It was sure quiet though here uptown, quieter than Corpus Christi. A trolley bumped up the tracks, the few passengers slumped down behind the lighted windows.

And Johnnie smacked headlong into a guy as tall as himself. He umphed, "Excuse me, Mister." Then he looked. For a minute he thought it was one of the Nazi-Rudamian peasants. It wasn't. The guy was a cop. "Excuse me," he repeated. "Should have been looking where I was going, sir. Guess I was too busy watching the street car." He kept stammering because he sure didn't want to be kept by a policeman right now. It was bad luck, that's what it was. The black cat with Magda's eyes.

The cop said pleasantly, "That's all right, soldier." In the dim light he appeared a good-looking dark fellow, not much older than Johnnie himself. His dark eyes were good-natured. But he didn't move out of Johnnie's way. "You on a furlough?"

"Just a pass."

"Live up this way?"

"No, sir. I'm from Texas. This is the first time I've ever been in New York."

The cop grinned. "How do you like it?"

"Well—I—" How did he like it? That hadn't occurred to him. He hadn't had time to think about New York at all. He hadn't even had time to see it. All at once he got mad. Not at the cop; he liked the guy's face. He'd always wished instead of yellow curly cowlicks he had black hair, not skimpy patent leather hair like Rudolph's but thick, like this fellow's would be from the looks of what showed under his cap.

"You don't like it?"

"Oh, I sure do!" Johnnie said quickly. "I always like new places. I'd never been out of Texas, only to Mexico, till I joined the Army. I've sure been enjoying all the strange places I've been seeing."

The cop grinned some more. "Glad you like it, soldier. It's my home town. Doesn't look the way it should because of the war. Wish you could have seen her when she was lit up. But then if it weren't for the war you wouldn't be here at all, would you?"

"That's right," Johnnie grinned back. He liked this young cop. Only he ought to be getting on his way. There wasn't much time left. "I haven't seen much of it yet but tomorrow—I guess it's today—anyhow I'm going to see the town, the whole town. The Empire State Building and Radio City and the Statue of Liberty and—"

"You should see the Bronx Zoo and the Metropolitan Museum, too. Sure most of the best pictures are sent away but there's the Roman Gardens—they're worth the price of admission. And the Egyptian tombs—" The cop broke off. He looked a little anxious, like Bill. "You'd better get going on your way now, soldier. It's not safe wandering around at nights any more." He shook his head sadly. "It used to be safe any time of the day or night up in these parts but it just doesn't seem to be since the brownout. You'd better get inside."

"Okay," Johnnie nodded.

" 'Night."

"Good night."

He started out but the cop turned after him. "Where are you stopping, soldier?"

"I don't know yet," Johnnie admitted. "My compadres are downtown waiting for me." He hoped. "Bill always takes care of things like that."

"How did you get so far uptown?"

"I came for a subway ride," Johnnie explained.

The cop doubled up. "That's a good one."

"Well, I wanted to," Johnnie defended. "Hank and Bill thought I was crazy but that's what I wanted to do."

"Pardon me for laughing," the cop apologized. "I couldn't help it. I live in the Bronx. Twice a day, every day, I'm a whole hour wasting time on the subway getting from and to home. I couldn't imagine anyone riding the subway for fun." He removed his cap now, brushed back the thick dark hair, just a little curly not like Johnnie's yellow bush. "Come on and have a cup of coffee with me just to show there's no hard feelings. Then I'll see you to your subway and you can go downtown to your friends."

"I'm not going downtown just yet," Johnnie said hesitantly. "There's no hard feelings only I haven't got time for a coffee. Wish I had but I'm late now."

"Where are you going?" A bit of suspicion went into that question.

Johnnie recited glibly, "The Dragham on West End Avenue."

"You know somebody there?"

"Oh yes," Johnnie nodded rapidly. "I don't know Edna Riggens—it's her apartment—but I know Rupe. He's the one I'm looking for."

"No trouble?" The cop wasn't suspicious but he was anxious again.

Johnnie laughed. "No, sir. I like Rupe." He closed his mouth quick. If he weren't careful he'd be talking too much. He brought his hand up vaguely. "Well, good night, sir. I sure enjoyed talking to you."

The cop settled his cap. "I might as well walk that far with you, soldier. Seeing's you're a stranger, you might get lost."

"You needn't do that," Johnnie assured him. "I never get lost. Except once in Newark and that was the parade."

"No trouble at all, soldier. I'm not looking forward to my subway ride." He haw-hawed on that, started Johnnie down the street.

You just couldn't tell a cop, "Run along, Bub," not even a cop off duty. Besides this fellow was nice. He talked kind of funny, sort of "dese" and "dose" and "goil," but so did most the New Yorkers he'd met at camp. Anyhow this cop was a regular Joe. He was trying to be helpful. He didn't know that Johnnie was mixed up with a mess of screwballs. If he, Johnnie, had had a guy like this with him tonight, he would have cleaned out that place hours ago, not wasted a good evening. For a moment Johnnie was inclined to tell all. He buttoned up his lip tighter. It wasn't going to do him any good in the Army if he got mixed up in a murder investigation. He would let Trudy take care of the police angle. She'd call them. She said she would.

"What's your name, soldier?" the cop asked chattily.

"Private First Class Johnnie Brown."

"How is it down in Texas? Lots of broncos and sage-brush and Indians?"

"Sure," Johnnie grinned. "What's your name?"

"Mike Costello."

"Say!" Johnnie shouted. "You played left end for

Fordham two years ago. Or are you that Michael Costello?"

The cop looked modest. "I'm the one."

"I was right end at Texas A. and M. last year. Not that I was in your class, Officer Costello."

"Call me Mike, Johnnie. We turn here."

They were on a long side street now. Almost pitch dark. Wasn't bad having someone beside you. Not that Johnnie was scared of the dark. But he liked company.

"Remember that game you played with N. Y. U.?"

"De Vi'lets," Mike Costello growled. "They spiked me in the first two minutes of play. I'll tell you how it was."

Johnnie hung on every word. He didn't even realize they'd been standing under the canopy of a mid-street apartment house until Mike concluded, "And that's why I scummed four of those gorillas—by accident, I mean. We always play clean. Well, here we are at the Dragham. You don't want me to wait and show you to the subway?"

"No, thanks," Johnnie said. "I'll be walking back with Rupe to his cousin's. I guess they'll see I find the right subway later." He clasped Mike Costello's hand. "I'm sure glad I bumped into you. I really did, didn't I? Anyhow it's something I'll always remember. My kid brother's going to get a big boot out of it when I write him I met Mike Costello of Fordham. Good night, Mike."

"Good night, Johnnie. Happy landings."

He strode back into the gloom. Johnnie peered into the dim foyer. This wasn't any dump. The lobby was full of over-stuffed furniture. In one chair there was a plum uniform with brass braid. The little guy in it nodded in snoring rhythm. Johnnie put his hand on the door. And suppose Rupe wasn't here? Who was he, Johnnie, to barge in on some strange woman at two o'clock in the morning? He took one long-legged stride back to the pavement. He spread his mouth wide with his forefinger and his little finger and he whistled. It sounded loud in the pitch quiet of West End Avenue. The murky figure down near the corner turned. Johnnie waved an arm wildly. Mike Costello came pounding back.

"What is it?" He asked. He wasn't a bit out of breath.

"Listen," Johnnie began. He barged right in without thinking of any consequences. "Listen, Mike, would you be interested in a murder?"

3.

Mike Costello leaned to him, smelled his breath. "I thought it was beer. It is beer."

"Only one beer," Johnnie said. "And the champagne was hours ago. I'm strictly sober."

"Didn't you say murder?"

Johnnie nodded.

"Here?"

"Oh no, not here. I haven't been here yet." Johnnie was polite. "I thought maybe if you aren't in too big a hurry to get home you might go in with me here to get Rupe, then we'll go back to where the murder is."

"And where is that?"

Johnnie's face fell. "I didn't even think. If Rupe isn't here I don't know how to get back." He rared up. "I've got to get back. She snitched my dog tags."

"Who's she?"

"Trudy. She's the one sent me after Rupe. And she took my dog tags so I'd come back."

Mike was patient. "What about this murder?"

"That's where it happened. In that house we're going back to—if Rupe's here."

"There really was a murder?"

"Yeah. Rudo and me found the body."

"Who is it?"

"A little guy named Theo. I don't know his last name."

"Who killed him?"

"I don't know," Johnnie said wide-eyed. "You're a policeman. I thought maybe you could find out. Trudy said she was going to call the police but I've been thinking maybe she won't. The whole bunch is pretty loopy. I think they're—"

Mike Costello sniffed again.

"I know it makes me sound loopy but I'm not," Johnnie defended. "Strictly not. You come along with me and I'll show you."

The cop said, "I ought to turn in an alarm if this is straight. Even if I am really off duty—I was just going to check out at my precinct when I met you. You say you don't know where this house is. How did you get there in the first place?"

"I followed a fat old man I saw on the subway. His name's Dorp. He was talking German and I didn't like it. It's his house. Listen, Mike, I have to hurry and get Rupe back before they take Rudo to the Clipper. I got to get my dog tags. You don't know that top sergeant of mine. I'll tell you all about it after we get Rupe."

Mike scratched his head. "Either you're stir crazy or giving me a rib is what I think, soldier."

"I'll prove it," Johnnie coaxed. "Will you come?"

Mike hesitated. "I might as well, Texas. Any guy with an imagination like yours needs a caretaker."

Johnnie sighed relief. "I sure hoped you would. And honestly every word is true."

They entered the foyer. Costello tapped the sleeping plum uniform on the knee. The little guy jumped up. When he recognized a cop he jumped again.

Mike asked, "What's that name, Johnnie?"

"Edna Riggens."

The little guy talked foreign. "What is it? I will call the manager, yes?"

"That you won't," Mike said. "You'll take us up to Edna Riggens' apartment and you won't call her either." He softened. "It isn't a pinch. We're pals."

Normal pallor returned to the man's face. "Yes. Yes indeed."

"Get going," Mike ordered. "Into the elevator with you. What's her number?"

"Ten B."

"That better be right."

"It is right."

"And we don't want any manager in this. So be sure you don't talk until we leave."

"Yes, sir," the man said sullenly. He stopped the cage at ten. "It is front left."

Johnnie stepped out first. Mike Costello followed. He said, "I ought to run that guy in on suspicion."

"Not now. We haven't time." Johnnie stopped at

B. "Listen, Mike, don't tell Rupe anything about the murder yet or he might not come with us."

"I won't," Mike swore. "I won't mention it to a soul." It was obvious that he still didn't believe it.

Johnnie pushed the button, kept his finger there. They waited. He didn't like this. Trudy didn't know Rupe was here. Edna wasn't going to appreciate getting out of bed at two in the morning for nothing.

The door opened with, "Hold your horses." The girl inside the darkened hall looked out at them and then she took another look, opening her brown eyes as big as plates. She was a honey. Upswept red hair, uplift black satin tight as a cinch. She smelled like whisky. Her voice wasn't pleasant when she said, "You got the wrong number, soldier." There was a Conga squawking away in the inner room. She yelled back, "Turn that damn thing off, Rupe."

"No, I haven't, babe," Johnnie grinned. He moved his foot inside the door.

"You sure have. I've never laid eyes on you before and you know it. Honestly, copper"—she dazzled a smile beyond Johnnie to Mike— "I've never laid eyes on him."

Johnnie heard Rupe's lazy voice coming behind her. "What's going on, Edna?" He came in sight. "It's Johnnie." He smiled all over his face. "It's my soldier boy, Edna." He brushed her out of the way. "Come on in, soldier. Bring your friend. Sure, come on. I've got just what you're looking for. Don't mind Edna, I pay the rent." He reached out, put his arm around Johnnie's shoulder. He spoke backward to Mike. "You come right along. Any friend of Johnnie's is my friend. Right here, soldier."

It was a nice living room with flowered couches and easy chairs and a big radio-phonograph. Edna followed reluctantly. Her eyes were still stretched wide. She picked up a half-filled highball glass and sat down plunk in the farthest away chair.

"Just what you're looking for, Johnnie. Help yourself." Rupe pointed to six bottles of champagne on the table. One was empty, one was being emptied. "Take one. More than I need. She doesn't like it."

"It makes me sick," Edna said through another gulp of whisky.

"You too," Rupe urged Mike. His face dripped sudden surprise. "It's a policeman!"

"Sure, it's a copper, Bright-eyes," Edna muttered.

"He's off duty," Johnnie explained. "He's Michael Costello—remember? Left end at Fordham. Officer Costello, Mr. Ruprecht."

"Pleased to meet you." Ruprecht bowed low. He teetered upward, urged, "Have a bottle. It's Ferenz' champagne, the best champagne." He raised his half-used bottle.

"We haven't time," Johnnie said. "We got to go."

"So sorry," Edna gritted. She took a bigger drink.

"You just arrived," Ruprecht complained.

"I came to get you. Trudy wants you."

Edna jumped up. "Who the hell is Trudy?"

"Trudy's his cousin," Johnnie said. "She needs him."

"Cousin, my eye-wash. He never told me about her." She went over to Rupe, put pointed black satin against him. "Don't go, Rupe. There's something damn funny about this. It smells."

Rupe disregarded her. "What does Trudy want?" He'd swung out of being tight fast enough, the way he had once before tonight.

"It's about Rudolph. They can't find the papers, the ones he has to have to go on the Clipper."

"I haven't them." Ruprecht felt in his pockets, shook his head. "Probably has them himself. One of his tricks."

"No, he hasn't," Johnnie stated out of knowledge. "It's serious. Mr. Lessering even left his party to come over."

"Not much of a party." Rupe lifted his eyebrows. "I left too."

"Trudy's been phoning all the night clubs for you."

"Dear Trudy." The redhead choked.

"Finally she asked me to go to the two places she couldn't phone to Hans'—"

"How is old Hans?" Ruprecht brightened. "I've neglected him. I'll have to go back to beer. I'm getting tired of champagne anyway."

"—and here."

"I have a phone," Edna bristled. "Why couldn't this dame phone?"

"You don't know Trudy, my sweet," Rupe soothed. "She'd never call me at a woman's. I might get the erroneous idea she cared."

Edna drew away. "That isn't healthy. If she's your cousin."

"Very distant. Under the rose perhaps." Rupe uptilted the bottle. "I'm afraid we had better go, Johnnie. If Trudy went to such lengths, even seeking a policeman—"

"She didn't send Mike," Johnnie explained quickly. "I found him myself."

"You're not taking him with us?"

Johnnie hesitated. "Well, yes I am. But it's for a different reason. You don't need to worry about that, Rupe."

"I doubt he'll be welcome," said Rupe sagely. His eyes narrowed slightly. "I doubt very much if he'll get in."

"I'll get in," Mike Costello announced with simple and menacing faith. "Don't worry about that, Bub. I'll get in."

Rupe shrugged. "If that is how you feel—" He took up his tall hat, his topcoat.

"You're walking out on me for this Trudy?" Edna shrilled.

"Time you were in bed anyway," Mike told her.

"If you do you needn't ever come crawling back here!"

Rupe spoke sweetly. "I never crawl, my pet. So undignified. But I'll be back. It may be years. It may be forever. But I shall return, my love."

"Get out!" She yelled. Johnnie was ready to duck but she didn't throw the glass.

Rupe said, "We mustn't forget the refreshments, Johnnie!" He returned to the table, held out two bottles to Johnnie, took the other two himself. "Good-by, my little dove. Until tomorrow. Alas, tomorrow never comes."

Her imprecations followed them to the elevator.

Five

RUPRECHT PUT A FINGER on the buzzer. "A sweet girl," he orated. "She is teaching me to Conga and Rhumba. Very good at it. Only she doesn't like champagne. Strange." He thrust a bottle at Mike Costello. "You wouldn't care to manage one for me? I thought not."

"Sorry, Bub. Not in uniform. Afraid I might run into Lieutenant McGonigle. Lefty, we call him."

The elevator took them down faster than it had brought them up. The operator didn't look at them.

"We'll have to go up to Broadway to find my car," Ruprecht pushed open the door to the street. "Or should I say Ferenz' car? I prefer that the chauffeur does not know all of my places of dalliance. Not that I enjoy walking. A highly overestimated form of travel."

"How'd you like to be a cop?" Mike asked.

"Would I get a whistle?" Ruprecht shook his head. "Not even for a whistle could I endure it. That is the trouble with all manly occupations—hunting, fishing, policemaning. Walk, walk, walk. And for what?"

Mike interrupted. "Do you know where this house is we're going to?"

"Dorp's, I presume."

"Texas here doesn't know the address."

"Hundred and Twelfth Street." Ruprecht scowled at Johnnie. "But you've been there. You just came from there."

"He came from Texas," Mike gurgled. "He didn't think to notice the address."

"I'd sure have been in a spot if you hadn't been at Edna's," Johnnie admitted. "I have to get back there. Trudy snitched my dog tags."

Rupe laughed admiringly. "Little devil."

"She did it so I'd come back. Though I don't know why she wanted me to come back particularly."

"You'll find women are like that," Rupe stated. "Especially Trudy."

They came over the crest on to Broadway.

"Gurk is somewhere about," Rupe said. "Perhaps a restaurant. If I could whistle now—"

Johnnie said, "I can." He did.

"There—up the block." Rupe took his hands away from his ears and pointed. The others followed his lead to the long black car. Gurk slept at the wheel.

"Don't the cops ever run him in for all-night parking?" Mike inquired.

"He has a host of good yarns. Try him sometime." Rupe rapped on the window. Gurk blinked, scrambled out to open the rear door. When he eyed Mike's uniform, his face retired.

"We are not arrested, my good man," Rupe said. He gestured his guests ahead of him, followed. "To Dorp's."

The car turned, cut across the tracks, headed uptown. It slowed to the corner of 112th Street. It stopped. A red lantern and a saw horse barred entrance. Two men held a drill. When they pressed it into the pavement it made an awful racket.

"This isn't the street," Johnnie said.

"Yes, it is."

Mike volunteered, "You don't know how fast the N.Y.C. street department can pop up, Johnnie. No use trying the other end. It's blocked too."

"Have to walk," Johnnie stated. He opened the door on his side. "It won't wear you down, Rupe. It's only half way down the block. You ought to be in the Army."

"That is a matter of opinion," Rupe said. "The Army takes the negative. I'm glad we brought refreshments. Dorp never has anything fit to drink. Stingy old coot." He patted the top hat slant on his head. "Lead on, my hearties."

They struck out for the house. It showed no light save the dimmed bulb in the lower hall. The throne room upstairs was completely blacked out. Johnnie had one foot on the steps when the voice from the gloom hit him.

"I wouldn't go in there, soldier," it said.

"Why not?" he demanded.

"I'm telling you."

Mike put in from the darkness below, "Are you the watchman?"

"Yeah, I'm the watchman," the man answered truculently.

"Watchman, what of the night?" Ruprecht mused.

"And I got my orders no one's to go in."

"Listen, you," Mike began.

"Wait, Mike." Ruprecht spoke up brightly. "It's the wrong house." He tittered. He nudged Johnnie with a champagne bottle. His voice was tighter than it had been. "You picked the wrong house." He nudged again. "It's the one next door we want."

Johnnie played up. "That's right." He'd forgotten. They were supposed to go in next door. He didn't know how Rupe knew it. "Sorry, Bud. We picked the wrong house. They all look alike in the dark."

"You mean that one?" The man jerked a thumb down the street.

"You aren't going to tell me we can't go in there?" Johnnie blustered. "I got a key. I'm supposed to go there."

Rupe interrupted quickly. "That's where I live. With my Aunt Gretchen. Good old girl, Gretchen. She always puts up soldiers on leave. She isn't home this evening. Aunt Bertha—she lives in Brooklyn—poor Aunt Bertha had another attack. But Aunt Gretchen told us to stay here just the same. Even gave us her key." He dangled the bottle. "Come on, men."

He lurched forward. Johnnie caught Mike's arm. "Come on."

Mike hung back. "What's up?"

"We got the wrong house," Johnnie said loud. He pushed Mike forward. "Come on." Into his ear he undertoned, "We can get in this other way. Don't say anything."

Rupe was climbing to the other door. "Where's the key, Johnnie? You didn't lose the key, did you?" He lowered his voice. "You really have the key?"

Johnnie stuck it in the lock. "Hurry up, Mike." Rupe was already in the hall. Johnnie pushed Mike, followed, closed the door tight. The three stood together in the black darkness. "We can't show a light," he warned.

"We'd better," Rupe said soberly. "Whoever put that fellow out there, he wasn't fooling. And he wasn't a watchman. We want him to think we're legal."

"I don't get it," Mike complained.

Rupe turned on a lamp. "Dorp uses both of these houses. But he does keep an old woman here for a front. Her name's Gretchen. She isn't here tonight. She's always sent to her sister's in Brooklyn when anything big is happening. That varlet couldn't know that Gretchen hasn't a nephew who sleeps in occasionally. Only we'd better get to Dorp's fast just in case he decides to report anything suspicious." He took a blackout torch from his pocket, turned it on the stairs. "Let's go up."

"What is happening here?" Mike demanded.

"Didn't Johnnie tell you?"

"I still think he's ribbing," Mike said. "All he told me was that a guy had been murdered."

"Murdered?" Rupe swirled too fast. Johnnie grabbed the banisters as Mike pitched into his backlegs.

"I told you not to tell him," Johnnie complained to the policeman.

"I forgot."

Rupe demanded. "Who is murdered?"

Johnnie spoke reluctantly. "Theo. The little punk who used to open the door."

Ruprecht scowled. "Why Theo?"

"It was supposed to be Rudolph."

"I knew it!" He started taking the steps, two at a time. The others scrambled after him in the darkness. There was no letup in pace until they reached the fourth floor attic room.

Mike panted, "You mean there actually was a murder?"

"Sure there was," Rupe retorted. "I'm surprised there hasn't been a massacre." He pulled on the overhead light here. The windows were painted over black. He

141

replaced his torch in his pocket, set the bottles of champagne on a rickety table.

The wall was solidly papered. It hadn't ocurred to Johnnie before he departed; he didn't know the trick of getting back in. He asked, "Shall we pound on the wall for Trudy?"

"Are you crazy?" Rupe demanded. "Someone else might be in there. No one must know I'm here."

"But they're waiting for you."

"In good time, soldier, all in good time. I don't want to be in the jug for a murder."

"Did you do it?" Mike asked quick.

"He wasn't here." Johnnie was disgusted. "He was with that Conga mouse."

Rupe was counting off bow-knots of wall paper. "But they'd like to pin it on me. And who has a better motive?" The wall began its slow angled swing.

"Will you look at that?" Mike gazed in awed admiration.

Rupe stepped back. "You take a squint, Johnnie?"

Johnnie advanced cautiously to the opening. He stepped through. The light had been left burning; the room was empty. He advised over his shoulder. "Coast's clear."

Ruprecht left the wall ajar as he followed. The befuddled Mike sniffed at the room. "Not very fancy," he commented.

"What do you expect in a guardhouse—pink ribbons?" Johnnie tried the door. Locked. He turned around. "What do we do now? Wait for Trudy?"

Mike came to life. "What's the matter with you dopes?

There's been a murder here." He rattled the knob. "It'll bust easy."

"There was a guard outside earlier," Johnnie warned.

"Listen. I'm the law." Mike stuck out his chest. "New York's finest."

"Off duty."

"In emergencies, always on duty. Murder's an emergency." He put his shoulder to the door.

"Wait!" Rupe cried.

"What for?"

"Why don't we take off the hinges? Then we can sneak up on them. No use bang-banging around. They might scram."

Johnnie examined the hinges. "This looks like a pipe."

"It is," Rupe agreed. "But it wasn't the first time I did it. Trudy's oiled it since then."

While Johnnie removed the pins, the others steadied the door.

"Now if you'll just smash the lock with your gun, copper, we can put it back together again and barge in and out easily."

"It's a pleasure," said Mike. He unbuckled his holster.

"Don't shoot!" Rupe warned. "Here." He took the gun, bumped it against the catch.

"One shot would do it," Mike complained. "And not so much noise either."

"You don't know how gun shy this house is," Rupe said solemnly. "There. That's enough."

Johnnie hadn't thought about that one. Somebody must have heard the shot that killed Theo. He hadn't.

And he'd been practically overhead. There were silencers. He'd read about them. But neither Magda's nor Trudy's gun was fitted. That cut out two who might have bumped off the underling. Not even those dames would be unsmart enough to walk up to someone in this house and say, "Let me take your gun with the silencer on it. I want to kill a guy."

The door was back on its hinges. "Now where's the stiff?" Mike wanted to know.

"Wait," Rupe called out again.

"What do you want us to do now?" Mike demanded. "Take up the floor?"

Ruprecht contemplated the rough boards. "A wonderful idea. Unfortunately it wouldn't let you down into the reception room." He glowed. "To be sure, if sweet Magda were in bed—" He shook his head dolefully. "She wouldn't be. You'd better use the staircase. You fellows are going downstairs."

"What about you?" Johnnie wanted to know.

"I'll make my entrance without fanfare. Later. You try to get word to Trudy, in private, that I'm here. I want a confab with her before I walk into Dorp's parlor. If you can't reach her, sneak back and let me know."

"And if I can't sneak back?"

"I will wait a reasonable length of time, soldier. After that I shall do it another way."

"You aren't going to run out?"

Ruprecht smiled. "I give you my word. I shall see it through. In fact it will give me great pleasure to see this through."

Johnnie had to take his word for it. He didn't exactly disbelieve Ruprecht's word. But if there should be any more shooting, any loud shooting, Rupe would be a sucker if he didn't take a powder. He and Mike were the only two who couldn't possibly have held the silent gun. Johnnie said, "Okay." He led Mike down the stairs quietly, pushed aside the trick closet wall.

Mike gasped. "Jeeze. It's like a film scarer, isn't it?"

"Wait'll you meet the folks," Johnnie whispered. He wished that he had had the cop with him when those S.S. guards were jerking around. Together they could have cleaned up the lot. Until Magda pulled the gun on both of them. He warned, "Keep quiet as you can, Mike. I want you to see the body before we walk in on them. This is the room here." Cautiously he made a light. "The body's over here—"

Mike asked, "Where?" His voice was flat.

Johnnie's eyes gazed hopelessly at the floor by the window. He said weakly, "It's gone."

Mike's face was hard-boiled. "Gone where?"

"It was here. Rudolph was in the closet, he didn't see it. I found it when I came over by the window. It was lying right down there on its face and the suitcase leaning against it. Like this—" He flung down on the rug, sprawled out. "With the hat like this—" He wrinkled his nose, stood up. "That floor smells funny."

"Blood?" Avid interest returned to the cop. He knelt, sniffed the boards beyond the rug. He stood up and brushed his knees. "Floor polish." His voice was flatter.

"Well, he was here," Johnnie insisted. "He sure was here." He didn't take to the I-was-right-about-this-all-the-time look on Mike's face. He scowled. "Those dirty Nazis have hidden him away. So they wouldn't have to report to the police. I knew they didn't mean to call the police." He suddenly saw it plain. "They didn't want Ruprecht here at all. They just wanted to get me out of the house so they could get rid of the body. Well, I'll show them."

He didn't wait for Mike; he pounded out of that room and down the stairs. How much noise he was making didn't matter. Not that it was much on the carpet. When he reached the throne room he flung open the doors belligerently.

They were all there, all looking pleased as hell over their trick. Rudolph was on the throne with the cigarette holder sticking out of his mouth. Magda and Ferenz were rallying round. Dorp and Ottomkopf sat on a squashy red velvet couch with Trudy between them. Janssen alone wasn't amused. He was gazing at Magda from afar and picking up the cigarette butts as they wafted down.

Johnnie spoke up loud. "Where's Theo?"

"Are you loose again?" Magda sighed. That was before her eyes popped like buttons. "The police," she breathed.

Each one of the others slowly, apprehensively turned eyes on Mike stepping up beside Johnnie. Every mouth rounded. "Police!"

Magda was the first to stop behaving like a spook. She came off the throne smiling, her hand outstretched. "How clever of you, Johnnie, to know just what we needed."

He didn't get it. This was such a complete nip-up, it dashed the temper out of him. It was pretty much of a surprise to most of the others too.

Magda stuck her hand right out in front of Mike. He had to take it. He didn't seem to mind. Well, in the yellow slacks and black coat she was something out of the glamour book. And the size of that ruby on her finger didn't spoil the picture. To think that he, Johnnie, had been dopey enough earlier to think that this bunch were merely jewel thieves. Magda was cooing, "Officer, it's so good of you to come. Officer . . .?"

"Mike Costello," the dumb cop smirked.

"Officer Costello, you don't know how we appreciate this, how relieved we are to have you here. It was sweet of Johnnie to bring you back to us. It is imperative that Rudolph reach the airport in time to take the Clipper."

Mike glinted real suspicion at Johnnie. Johnnie opened his mouth but Magda lifted her voice. "We didn't see how we could make it without an escort—"

"You want a motorcycle cop, lady," Mike stated. He glowered at Johnnie again before giving Magda the alert.

Johnnie shouted before she could sabotage any longer, "Where's Theo?"

Dorp beamed, "What do you want with Theo? He has gone home."

"He couldn't go home."

"He has," Dorp nodded. "He was tired. He lives so far, all the way to Queens he has to go. After I dismiss the attendants, I say Theo too may leave us early."

"Dead guys can't walk," Johnnie stated distinctly.

Magda raised impatient eyebrows. "What are you talking about?"

"Theo was dead."

"Dead? Was dead?"

"He was dead. Maybe he was going home but somebody killed him before he got out."

They were all closing in on him now, all but Rudolph who kept right on lounging on the throne, and Janssen who had to stand by to pick up the butts.

"When was this?" Dorp asked curiously.

"Before I left. I found him. I told you about it. I—"

"Where?"

"You might as well stop this game," Johnnie began.

"Where?" Dorp repeated.

"Upstairs. In Rudolph's room—Trudy's room—"

Ferenz smiled magnificently. Dorp began to laugh. At least that was what it was supposed to be. Johnnie figured that out because the mouth turned up. Trudy just stood there upping big eyes at him.

Magda cried, "You must be crazy! There's no one in Rudo's room."

"Not now there isn't," Johnnie interrupted loudly. "But there was—"

He saw Mike's grim mouth and he raised his voice louder. "You're darn right there was. He was lying on his face by the window and he was dead as a duck." He broke through the circle toward the throne. "You tell them, Rudo. You saw him too."

"Saw whom?" Rudolph squeaked airily.

"Theo. Up in your room. Murdered."

The princeling drew himself up. "I never saw anything of the sort," he denied flatly. His black eyes looked smack into Johnnie's. "How silly!"

2.

Johnnie didn't say any more. He just looked at Rudolph. Looked at him and didn't believe his ears. He turned around slowly. They were all watching him. But they weren't surprised or annoyed like they were pretending. Underneath that they were all making mock of him. All but the cop. Mike was really mad.

Johnnie came up for the third time spying the lifesaver. "Trudy," he began.

She shook her head. She turned sweetly to Mike. "I don't know why he's saying this, officer. As a matter of fact, we don't even know who he is. He walked in here tonight—"

Ferenz broke in. "He even crashed a party of mine tonight, officer." He puffed up. "I am Ferenz Lessering. No one crashes my parties."

Mike was sure by now that Johnnie had hoaxed him. He didn't like it. But he didn't not like it as much as he would have if Magda's cheek hadn't been practically against his arm.

Johnnie took a deep breath. "All right," he announced. "All right," he repeated. He fixed reproachful eyes on Mike. "You can believe these birds if you want to. I've told you what they are. Go ahead and believe them. You're going to look pretty funny after you come to." He butted through that circle as if it were not there.

Magda carolled after him, "Where are you going now, Johnnie?"

"I'm going to find Theo!" he howled back.

He heard Mike as he started down the stairs. "I better

go along to see he doesn't hurt anything," and Magda's laughter, "He can't hurt a thing."

He gritted his teeth. He'd tear this house down wall by wall before he'd let them get by with this. He'd start searching at the bottom. Someone was following him down the stairs. Johnnie swung around and doubled his fists.

Mike halted. "Now listen, Johnnie—"

"You listen," Johnnie said. "I tell you somebody killed this guy Theo and now somebody's hidden the body so the police won't find it." He scorned. "Though why they think the police would be interested, I don't know."

"Listen, Johnnie—"

"You listen." He pounced again. "Rudolph saw that body and he told them about it, not me. And no one was surprised either." He cocked his head. "Get that. They knew Theo was dead the minute Rudolph and me walked in. Because Rudolph was the one supposed to be dead. Theo was the only one who looked like Rudolph."

"Listen, Johnnie." Mike raised his voice. "Listen just for a minute, will you? Why would a guy be killed just because he looked like another guy?"

"Because somebody doesn't want Rudolph to go back and be king."

"King?" Mike backed up a few steps. Johnnie guessed they'd told him that he, Johnnie, was kind of cuckoo.

"Yes, king!" he snapped. If Mike couldn't tell who was crazy in this outfit and who wasn't there was no time now to go into it. "That Rudolph's a prince. A crown prince of Rudamia. You never heard of it and neither did I but it's a place near Trudamia and Luxembourg only the Nazis own it now."

Mike came down to him. He coaxed, "Listen, Johnnie, let's—"

"I'm giving it to you straight. Ask Rudolph. He won't lie about that. He wants to be king." He wondered. "Magda wants him to be king because she's going to marry him. That'll make her a queen. Ottomkopf—that's old bristle-head—wants him to be king because he'll get to boss Rudamia." He confided, "Rudolph's kind of a goon." He thought about it again. "Ferenz wants him to be king because Rudolph owes Ferenz a lot of money and he could pay off then. But if Rudolph was killed, Ruprecht would be king. And Magda'd rather have Rupe. Only she hasn't got him. I wonder. If Rupe wanted to be king, he might bump off Rudo, only Rupe doesn't want to be and he's the one guy couldn't have done it. He wasn't here."

"Maybe he only just got to Edna's," Mike suggested. "Maybe she's just his alibi."

"She was mad enough to spill if that was it," Johnnie stated. "Trudy says she doesn't want Rupe to be king. She goes for him though and she might be lying." She'd lied in his face. Saying she would call the police. Good thing he had a hunch. "She might think she could beat Magda out. She could with me. I don't know where Dorp comes in it. He's trying to get Rudolph off on the plane. Dorp's a Nasty. He has his own S. S. troops."

Mike stopped believing again.

"Didn't you get that suit on Janssen? There was a whole squad of them here earlier. Bowing and scraping. Your Highness this. Your Highness that."

"Listen, Johnnie, there aren't any more kings," Mike reasoned. "Except in England and Abyssinia—"

"That's what I thought, brother, until tonight. But there is a Rudamia. It's in the Encyclopaedia Britannica. And that goop upstairs is going to be king of it. If he lives so long." He caught Mike's lapel. "Don't you see we got to find out who did it before Rudolph does get killed? And first we have to find Theo. They can't lie out of a murder if we find Theo." He put it down cold. "Are you going to help me look for him or not?"

Mike scratched his nose. "If you're talking straight —I'm not saying I believe you, see?—but if it should be true all this stuff about kings and about you finding a stiff, you don't think they've got it hidden here, do you?"

"Where else?"

"If they thought you could find the body—I mean, supposing there really is one—you don't think they'd turn us loose to look for it, do you? There's more of them than of us."

"But you're a cop—they couldn't stop you looking."

"Yes, they could," Mike said slowly. "Murderers aren't particular about who they put the second bullet in. You can't go to the chair more than once."

Johnnie deflated. "What do you think we ought to do?"

"I think we ought to go report to Ruprecht."

"I think so too," Trudy's voice agreed. She was sitting there above them on the stairs.

"How long have you been there?" Johnnie demanded.

"Long enough." She stood up, shook out her pink slacks' creases. "You did bring Ruprecht back?"

"Yes, I brought him back."

"Then come on. Take me to him."

Johnnie didn't move. "I'm looking for Theo."

"You won't find him here," she said. "And I must see Ruprecht before the others do. I told them I'd follow you and see you didn't get into any mischief. And I told them they'd better stay put because you might get suspicious if all of them trailed you around. Now take me to Rupe."

"Where's Theo?" Johnnie demanded stubbornly.

"Have you tried Queens?" she mocked.

"Kings—queens—"

"Shshsh. Do you want all of them down here? Officer Costello, will you take me to wherever Rupe is holed? Johnnie can stay here and play hide-and-seek all he wants. I must see Rupe right away."

"You better come with us, Johnnie," Mike urged. "I think we ought to talk this over with Rupe."

He gave in. "All right. He's up in the attic where you had me."

Trudy nodded. "Be quiet both of you. We'll go up. Wait—Officer Costello—"

"Call him Mike," Johnnie said. "No use being formal with a cop."

"Mike, why don't you go back in with the others? Tell them I'm following Johnnie around. That way if any of them do start looking for us you can give a warning. I don't want them to see Rupe yet."

"Rupe didn't want to be seen yet," Mike admitted. He was torn between a possible body and Magda's figure. "I don't know—"

Trudy nodded her butter yellow head. "It'll be safer."

"How can I signal you?"

"Shoot your gun," Johnnie advised. "Though I don't know if we'd hear it upstairs. I didn't hear the shot that killed Theo."

"After you shoot it, be sure you're in the lead if anyone comes after us." She gave Mike her Sonja smile. "You go first now. We'll wait until you're safe inside."

"Okay," Mike agreed. "But come back and let me know what you decide, Johnnie."

"Don't worry." He wasn't going to lose the cop after finding him. He stood behind Trudy on the stairs until Mike had shut himself in the throne room.

She whispered, "Come on now. Don't talk until we get upstairs." On third she turned again. "You lamebrain. Why did you bring that cop here?"

"I thought he might come in handy," Johnnie told her. "Why did you lie about Theo?"

"What did you expect me to do, tell Mike all about it? Don't you think I have enough on my mind without you bringing home a policeman?"

"Mike's a good guy. Besides you told me you'd call the police and you didn't. You're not going to get away with murdering Theo by hiding him."

"I didn't murder Theo," she retorted. "And I'm not trying to get away with anything." She pushed open the secret closet door. "I wish I knew who did it." She smelled like lemon perfume here in the dark. He caught hold of her hand, just for guidance.

"Listen, if you'd tell Mike there was a murder," he said, "he could find out. After all he is a cop."

154

"He can find out after I get Rudolph away from here."

"Suppose Rudolph did it?"

She was disgusted. "He didn't. He's the one person didn't. He could never have mistaken Theo for himself." She opened the door of the attic. Her mouth turned down at the corners. "He's gone."

"He said he wouldn't run out," Johnnie frowned. "Try tapping on that phony wall."

"You watch at the door." She tapped, called softly, "It's Trudy."

The wall swung a little, wider. Ruprecht came in.

"I thought maybe you'd blown," Johnnie sighed.

"Such lack of confidence!" Ruprecht scoffed.

"Rupe!" Trudy cried. That was the first time Johnnie realized that she wasn't as tough as she'd been acting. She sort of caved in against Ruprecht's chest. He kissed her, none of the lingering stuff he'd given Magda in the library, just a nice big brother kiss.

"What's the matter, sweet stuff?"

"Oh, Rupe. So much."

Johnnie said, "Pass me a chair, Rupe. My feet hurt. I'll guard sitting down." He put it against the door, plopped on it.

Ruprecht and Trudy parked on the table. She wailed, "Somebody's trying to kill Rudolph."

He nodded. "Johnnie told me. About Theo."

"That wasn't all. Before that Dorp gave Theo an envelope. And he said Rudo wasn't to reach Rudamia. I stole it. But there's nothing wrong with it. Just his real passports."

For the first time in hours, Johnnie remembered the

bomb cigar in his pocket. Remembered it none too comfortably. Time was getting on. It was set to go off on the Clipper. He didn't know exactly what time the Clipper was leaving but it might be dangerously close.

"They think you have it, Rupe."

"Give it to me then. I will have it." He put his arm around her shoulder.

She leaned her head against him. "I haven't it here. It's in the little room, under the uniforms in the wardrobe."

"I'll get it. You say there's nothing wrong with it?"

"Not a damn thing, Rupe."

That envelope wouldn't have just killed Rudolph. It would have killed all the passengers, everyone on board the Clipper. Johnnie sat up. Maybe it was meant to kill everyone. Maybe even the president would be on board. "Say," he began.

They didn't pay any attention to him. They were pitching a little quiet woo during this conference. Well, he, Johnnie, didn't blame Rupe for making time. He merely envied him.

"Rupe, I don't think we ought to let Rudolph leave on the Clipper," Trudy said.

"I thought you wanted it, baby. You even told me to stay out of the picture so that there wouldn't be any chance of me rubbing Rudo the wrong way and making him change his mind."

"I know. It did seem like a good idea when Furry first told me of it. Before someone tried to kill Rudolph."

"You know," Ruprecht smiled winningly, "I can

think of a lot of persons who would like to kill Rudolph for any number of reasons. But there isn't a one of them in this house. That's what I don't get. On the face of it, everyone here should want Rudolph to be king. It's the only way for Magda to get in the ranks. If Furry was losing money on such a deal, he might do it, but in the long run he isn't. Or if Otto were going to get kicked out on his pratt, but Rudo wouldn't dare."

"That's the way I figure," Johnnie interrupted. They still weren't paying any attention to him. Ruprecht was tugging her curly yellow hair and she was rubbing his knee.

"Someone doesn't," Trudy said. "And that's why I don't think we ought to let him leave. If he isn't even safe here with his friends, he certainly won't be in Europe."

"What'll we do with him?" Rupe brightened. "Maybe Edna would like to hide him."

"Who's Edna?"

"Madame La Riggens. My Conga teacher."

"She stinks."

"But sweetly. What do you think we ought to do with him?"

"We could turn him over to the state department."

Ruprecht scowled. "I don't think he'd want to be interned."

Trudy shook her head. "He'd love it, Rupe. The best food and wine. Nothing to do but play cards and gossip in a beautiful hotel. I think it's a perfect solution."

Ruprecht bit her cheek absently. "Maybe you're right. But come the revolution, who gets to be king?"

He kissed her just as absently. Johnnie made a face. If a guy was going to kiss a honey like Trudy, he ought to have his mind on his work.

"That's just it," she said briskly. "I don't think there's going to be any revolution. Not until after the war. I think Dorp's lying about Rudamia turning on Hitler. They wouldn't have the nerve. I think that's all a part of the gag to get rid of Rudolph. But if it should be true—" She took his hand, patted it. Her voice was sugary. "Why not let Kraken be president?"

"What!"

"Why not, Rupe?"

"What about me?"

She stuck out her chin. "You don't want to be king, do you?"

"God, no! You know I don't."

"You don't need to be king. You have plenty of money without being king. There's all that money your Uncle Isaiah from Chicago left you."

"It's in trust until I'm thirty. I only get the income. It's not enough to keep me in champagne."

"Too bad," she scowled. "Well, if you had to, you could go to work at some more pleasant job than king-ing, couldn't you?"

"Ye-es."

"Then why not? If Rudolph gets back on the throne before he's assassinated, you'll have to be king. You're it." She coaxed pretty again. "But if neither of you go back then Kraken will take over as soon as Rudamia can run the Nazis out."

Ruprecht said, "I don't like Kraken."

"How do you know you don't? You never exchanged

a word with him except, 'Saddle the black mare' or 'Curry the stallion.' You might like him a lot if you ever stood him a beer at Hans!" She quirked a smile. "I always thought he was sort of cute."

Rupe grabbed her shoulders. "Trudy! You didn't ever go out with him?" He shook her. "That night I met you coming in about one o'clock—the night you went to bed early with a headache—"

"Don't be silly," she said sweetly, and eagerly, "How about it, Rupe?"

Maybe Ruprecht believed her; he gave her a cigarette. Johnnie wasn't such a dope. She hadn't denied it; she'd wiggled.

"What about you?" Rupe demanded.

"What about me?"

"I always thought—I mean—I rather took it for granted you'd marry me some day."

Johnnie's eyes blinked. He'd never sat in on a proposal before. It was kind of embarrassing. Only the others seemed to have forgotten that he wasn't just a decoration on the door.

"How sudden," Trudy blew out smoke.

"Don't be an ass."

"I won't." She sighed. "But if you ever do want to propose, that won't make any difference. Mum and I aren't going back to Trudamia."

"No?"

"No. Mum's bought an inn in Switzerland. She's running it and making pots of money. There's a dairy farm went with it and she's having the time of her life making butter and cheese. You know she always liked to churn. I sort of think she's going to marry the former innkeeper. She says he has the sweetest whiskers. **Anyway she's not going back to Trudamia. And neither am I.**"

"What are you going to do?"

She said, "I don't know," but he didn't take the **hint.** "I know one thing though. I'm going to be an **American.** After all, my father was a naturalized one. So you see you won't have to be a prince when you get around to marrying me. And we can keep Rudolph from being king."

Ruprecht nodded somberly. "Maybe," he said. "Have you thought of consulting Rudolph on this?"

She shook her head.

"You know of course that he may want to be king."

"He does, drat him. That's why you had to come here. You've got to change his mind."

"My God, Trudy," he groaned. "Change Rudolph's mind?"

"Well, maybe not that," she admitted. "But you have to think of something to delay him, to keep him from going on this Clipper. You do that much and leave the rest to me."

He rumpled her hair. "That bodes no good, fair one. The first time I left all to you I lost my eyebrows. Remember that infernal chemical set you had when you were sweet seven? And the last time as I recall, I was fired out of Yale for leaving all to you. Why did you tell the Proctor you were a bubble dancer?"

"He wouldn't believe I was Crown Princess of Trudamia."

Johnnie was on his feet, his back against the door. "I hate to interrupt but someone's just started up the stairs. Two people."

Ruprecht kissed Trudy on the mouth. There was nothing casual about that one. "I'll get the papers and bust in. Clean this room fast as you can." He was behind the wall like magic.

Trudy beckoned to Johnnie. "Come over here and hold my hand."

He made it in two and a half strides. He didn't waste time hand-holding though. He went into a clinch. He deserved a kiss himself. He didn't break it until he heard the door open.

3.

Trudy said under her breath, "Why, Johnnie Brown!" Her eyes were laughing.

Magda and Mike stood on the threshold. Magda's eyebrows were up like flags. "Have you found the body?" She inquired with a leer in those green eyes.

"Not yet," Johnnie admitted.

Trudy spoke pertly. "We haven't looked in your room, darling."

"Why not," she countered.

"I'm always afraid of what I might find there." Trudy cooed. She slid from the table. "Come on, Johnnie, let's go down and have a drink." She said regally to Magda, "You may have the sofa now."

Magda disdained. "I don't want it. Mike and I were merely curious, you were gone so long. He didn't know you'd—taken time off."

Mike was panting to ask questions. It was all over his face. Johnnie tried to give him the high sign. He hoped it caught. He urged, "Come on, Mike. Trudy's been telling me about Trudamia. Sounds like a swell

161

country. You ought to tell Mike about that time you were caught sneaking in the palace after hours."

Magda's mouth narrowed. "Instead of such fantasies, Trudy, you might be trying to locate Ruprecht. There isn't much time before we must leave for the Clipper."

"He'll be here." Trudy managed to shoo everyone out ahead of her, close the door with a double bang. "I told you—or were you and Rudolph too busy talking? —that woman said she'd send him right over."

"What woman?" Magda demanded.

Trudy smiled. "His dancing teacher, darling. She has the loviest dyed red hair."

"You're making it up." Magda banged through Theo's room, started down to second.

"Oh no, I'm not," Trudy yelled after her. "I could do a lot better than that if I were making it up!"

Ferenz met them at the throne-room door. "I wish you girls would stop running all over the house with these strange young men. Rudolph feels neglected."

Johnnie and Mike swelled out their chests.

"Besides it's getting late and we still don't have those papers. Where is Ruprecht?"

"He'll be here any minute now," Trudy assured him.

Rudolph was off the throne. He sulked at Magda. "It took you long enough to find her."

Johnnie looked quick at Mike. Mike winked. Johnnie grinned. But it occurred to him he might have played the wrong number tonight in Trudy. She was in love with Ruprecht. Whereas Magda wasn't in love with Rudolph, and she wasn't that in love with Ruprecht. Only trouble there was that Magda scared him off. It took a real New Yorker like Mike to handle that babe, somebody used to swell dishes.

Dorp pattered through the inner doorway. "I have made liverwurst sandwiches and some coffee as you suggest, Ferenz." He spied Trudy. "And where have you been, Miss? It gets later and where is Ruprecht?"

"He'll be here any minute," she likewise reassured him.

"What do you say we all eat?"

Rudolph said, "I want a bowl of chile."

"We'll get that for you at the airport." Ferenz patted him. "Let's have some nice sandwiches and coffee now."

"And cake," Dorp added.

Rudolph stuck out his lip. "I don't want sandwiches and coffee. I don't want cake. I want chile."

Ferenz' eyes glittered. "There is no chile."

"Some house with no chile," Johnnie put in. Evidently he'd missed one of the prince's tantrums. One good break. "Back home in Texas you'd as lief run out of soap as chile. Liefer."

"Texas," Rudolph breathed. "Did you say Texas?"

"Yeah," Johnnie defied him. "I said Texas."

"I was in Texas," he sighed. "Days and days—"

"I said Texas." Johnnie walked right up to him. "I come from Texas. You want to make something out of it?"

"Not now!" Ferenz shrilled.

Ottomkopf glowered, "Why is this man loose again?"

"Ask Trudy," Magda smiled.

"Why shouldn't he be?" Mike joined Johnnie.

Johnnie swung to him. "I didn't tell you they tied me up twice tonight, did I? That's the kind of a bunch this is, tying a soldier of Uncle Sam's. Would you have believed that?"

"Officer, can't you take this man into custody?" Ferenz begged. "He is definitely insane. A persecution complex."

"Why don't you throw me out?" Johnnie demanded.

"Why don't you?" Rudolph urged.

Ferenz didn't answer those.

"Why don't you, Rudolph?" Ruprecht drawled from the doorway. He was tight again or acting tight. He'd put on his top hat and he had one hand stuck behind his tails. In his other hand he held out an envelope, a fat white envelope blobbed with red sealing wax.

"The papers!" Ferenz gurgled. "Ruprecht, I could kiss you!"

"Not without getting your teeth knocked out," Ruprecht grinned. "You mean this?" He waggled the envelope out of reach.

"Yes, dear. We've been waiting for that. Where did you get it?"

"Found it," Rupe teetered.

"Where?" Dorp demanded.

"Under Magda's pillow."

"That's a lie!" she cried.

"That's a lie," Rudolph echoed. "You're just trying to make me jealous."

"I didn't say Magda was under the pillow," Rupe grinned. "Just this."

"It isn't true!" she said. "If it was there, someone put it there. And what were you doing in my room?"

Rudolph echoed again, "What were you doing in her room?"

"I always go first to Magda's room. Just to see what's going on. Dull tonight. Who wants this moldy old envelope?" He held it out of reach from the advance.

"I will take it," Dorp decided firmly. He did.

Ruprecht brushed off his hands, stuck them into his pockets. "Hello, Gorgeous," he greeted Magda.

"It's been opened," Dorp said softly.

"Sure, it's been opened," Ruprecht admitted. "Wanted to see what was inside."

The fat man's voice was dangerous. "What did you do with the rest of it?"

"What rest of it? That's all there was, there wasn't any more." He winked at Trudy. "Hello, Snookums."

Ferenz began softly, "Concentrate, Ruprecht. Please, dear." He put his hand on Rupe's arm. "For old Furry. Think hard. What did you do with the rest of it?"

"Nothing else."

"Let me see it." Ferenz tore it away from Dorp, ruffed through the papers. "What is it missing?"

"Should I know?" Dorp shrugged. "I saw only the outside of it. But when I received it from Herr Ottomkopf, it was more thick, more heavy."

Ottomkopf didn't stir a bristle on his head.

Janssen chimed in. "Yes it was. Herr Ottomkopf, you look. What is it missing from the envelope?"

Ottomkopf said, "I did not prepare the envelope. I received it. I passed it on. That is all."

"What's supposed to be in it?" Trudy asked.

Johnnie spoke out of the corner of his mouth to Mike. "There's coffee going to waste. I could use a cup." He edged away from the group. Mike followed. No one yapped at them.

They went down the room and into the next. It was the swellest dining room Johnnie had ever seen. The walls were all tapestry, guys in wigs and skirts hunting with spears. The table and chairs must have been built right here. They were too heavy to carry around. The swellest part was the big coffee pot with steam and smell exuding from it, the platter of sandwiches, the dish of cakes. Johnnie stuffed a pink one into his mouth while he poured two cups. He said, "I'm dead on my feet. No sense of our listening to that ring around the rosy. The guy who really knows what was in the envelope isn't going to talk."

Mike double-decked a sandwich. "What do you suppose is missing?"

"I know what's missing," Johnnie said. "And I'm the only one knows except the guy who put it there."

"What is it?"

"A bomb."

Mike swallowed half a sandwich without chewing. "A bomb!"

"Shshsh." Johnnie went to the door, peeked out. The whole bunch was arguing now. "Don't let them hear you say that. I might get in trouble."

"How do you know it's a—cupcake?"

"Because I'm the guy who opened the envelope. Trudy passed it to me after she lifted it. I'm the guy who took out the—cupcake."

"What did you do with it?"

"It's in my pocket."

Mike smiled and laid himself back in the chair. "Who you kidding?"

"All right, wise guy." Johnnie wiped his fingers on

the tablecloth. "Look." He edged it out of his pocket, one eye on the door. "There she is. There's the cupcake."

Mike was suspicious. "Looks like a cigar to me."

"Sure it does. But I've had a course on bombs. This is the kind automatically ignites at a certain time. Of course you can pull the pin and make it go off sooner."

"You hadn't ought to carry it around in your pocket like that."

Johnnie manfully put it back in. "I think it's safe. You see, it couldn't be meant to go off here. That would get the guy who made it. It must have been safe in the envelope until Rudolph was on the Clipper." He took another sandwich to keep his stomach from playing scales. "Anyhow don't you say anything about it yet."

"I won't. But I think I better call up the precinct and get some help over here. Fast."

Johnnie chewed gravely. "I don't think they'll let you borrow the phone. They killed Theo you know."

"You really did see him?"

Johnnie scowled. "You mean you still don't believe it?"

"By now I don't know what I believe." Mike drank his coffee black. "I should have gone to bed instead of trying to play Boy Scout to you."

Johnnie jumped up suddenly. He grabbed a nut-studded cupcake and began eating fast. "I got it, Mike!"

"Got what?"

"I know where Theo is."

"Where?"

"That's it." Johnnie nodded his head wisely. "That's just it."

"Well, tell it."

He lowered his voice. "Those guys cutting up the street. They're not from the Street Department. They're Dorp's men. They're digging up the street for Theo. Put him in the hole. Close it up. Theo never shows again."

Mike shook his head. "Where could they get a drill?"

"Where did they get those Nazi uniforms? And a bomb? Getting it wouldn't bother them any. Mike—" He grabbed another cake quickly. "We've got to stop them before it's too late."

"If they aren't going to let me phone, you think they'd let you go out and stop those men?"

Johnnie hadn't considered that. "We aren't going to tell them," he figured. "We'll say we're going to look for Theo. They don't care how much we look for him in this house. Then when we get downstairs we'll make a dash for the door. Once outside if that watchman starts anything, I'll let him have it. You have a gun and a police whistle, haven't you? And I have a couple of fists."

"Okay, soldier. Let's go."

Johnnie took another cake with him for reinforcement. They marched back into the throne room. The bunch was still arguing. Rudolph had collapsed on the throne. Janssen was rallying on one side, Magda on the other. They could dig each other without the goon catching on. Ferenz and Ottomkopf, Dorp and Trudy were doing most of the talking. But loud. Ruprecht alone was out of it. He was balancing his silk topper on his nose. He inquired, "Where did you go to, soldier?"

"I was hungry. There's a lot of good grub going to waste in there."

"Lead the way." He clapped the hat over one ear and put his arm through Johnnie's.

Johnnie pointed. "Right down there at the end of the room to the right. You can't miss it."

"I might," Ruprecht insisted. "You show me."

"We can't show you now," Mike said. "We got to—"

"Aw, come on, show me first. Won't take a minute. What's so important?"

"We have to find Theo," Mike said.

"He won't run away," Ruprecht argued.

Johnnie began to catch on. Rupe wasn't tight any more than he'd been earlier. He had something he wanted to say. Privately. "All right, I'll show you. Come on."

Mike started after them until Magda cooed, "Officer Costello."

Mike looked at her then he looked at Johnnie.

"Go on," Johnnie said. "See what she wants."

She didn't look as if she wanted anything more than a little variety. But whatever she wanted would be worth investigating.

Ruprecht waited until they were in the dining room. "Do you have a gun?" he demanded.

"No, I don't."

"Damn nonsense. I left mine at home. I didn't expect any trouble." He poured a cup of coffee, swallowed it quickly.

"Mike's got one," Johnnie said. "So has Magda and Trudy and—"

"—everyone else that shouldn't have. There's trouble ahead."

"What kind of trouble?"

"Fighting trouble. Dorp says Rudolph can't leave without the missing papers. Ferenz says whatever is missing could be sent to him in Switzerland. He also points out that he can't arrange a seat on the Clipper every day. Magda agrees with Ferenz. So does Rudolph."

"What does Old Bristle-Head say?"

"Ottomkopf? He's too mad to say anything. First he sides with Dorp and then he sides with the others. And he wants to know who let a soldier and a policeman in here. What he wants most is to take a rubber truncheon to me. I say that's all the thanks I get for finding their damn papers. Trudy's trying to organize a search of the house. Stalling for time. I think she knows what's missing. I think she hid it purposely."

Johnnie didn't know whether to mention the bomb or not. If he did, Ruprecht might take it away from him to use as his weapon. Johnnie sort of liked having it in his pocket. If he finally had to fight his way out of here, it would come in handy. He didn't mention it. Instead he asked, "What do you want a gun for?"

"Because I want to use it if the final decision is for Rudolph to leave. He's an ass but after all he is my brother. And I don't go for having him killed by the Nazis."

Johnnie thoughtfully selected another cake. He wasn't hungry but it was something to do and for free. "I think we all need guns," he said. "I mean you and me and Mike and Trudy. I think Dorp's a Nazi and I think those soldiers of his are Nazis too. I don't know why he wants to kill Rudolph only if he does, he's going to kill you too."

"Kill me?" Ruprecht echoed quietly.

"Figure it out for yourself. Who takes over if anything happens to your brother?"

Rupe figured it. "Could be that the Nazis want that damn Kraken to take over. I don't doubt a bit that he's gone whole hog for the New Order. Ugly bastard. But why would Trudy play Dorp's game?"

"Maybe she doesn't know."

"Why do you think we've had her and Magda living here but to keep an eye on Dorp? And who got me over here tonight? I had no intention coming into it. I'll talk to Trudy. She has a gun?"

"Yeah." He looked at Rupe's face anxiously. "You wouldn't hurt Trudy, would you?"

"I'd beat her to a pulp if I thought she was selling me out." He didn't look as if he were fooling. Johnnie followed fast.

Mike and Magda alone occupied the throne room. They were gazing into each other's eyes. Magda was gold and black wickedness. Mike was pleased.

"Where's Trudy?" Ruprecht demanded.

"They've all gone hunting, darling. Want a drink?"

"Where's Rudolph?" Johnnie shouted. "Who let Rudolph go? You know someone's trying to kill him."

"Don't be silly," Magda deprecated.

"Come on," Johnnie called. He ran to the door. Mike ran after him.

"He's safe," Mike said. "They went in pairs. He's with Trudy."

Johnnie slowed down and breathed again. "As long as we're started," he decided, "we might as well get outside before they finish the search. If you can tear yourself away from Yellow-britches."

Mike did look sheepish. "On her they aren't repulsive," he said. "We're going to look pretty silly if that's the N. Y. C. street department outside."

"You're going to look sillier if Theo has to be dug out of the street again."

They reached the foot of the stairs.

"After we're out, how we going to get back in?" Mike asked.

"We're coming back with the whole force," Johnnie boasted. "And Theo. Though personally I'd just as lief not see this place again. If I only had my dog tags—" He had his hand on the doorknob before he remembered to look toward the chenille curtains. He wouldn't have been surprised if the whole outfit was lined up there poking guns on him. He was exceedingly surprised that the curtains didn't even quiver. "Outside, brother," he warned Mike.

It was that easy. They descended the steps, headed toward the drill in the middle of the street. Mike let him take the lead. Either Mike was still afraid he'd look silly or his mind was on that green-eyed thing back in the house. The drill made a worse noise than the Louisiana maneuvers. Johnnie set his teeth.

The two workmen took a recess when he upped to them. He demanded, "What are you doing here?"

The one with his hat pulled over one eye said nastily, "Playing gin rummy. Want to set in?"

The one with his hat over both eyes said, "What do you think we're doing, wise guy?"

You couldn't distinguish faces, not on a black night in a brownout. They didn't need the hats to hide them.

Johnnie persisted, "Why are you digging up this street?"

"We like to dig up streets," the first guy said. "Any objections?"

"I want to know why you're digging it up now at this time of the morning."

They eyed each other.

"Drunk," the first worker said.

"Nuts." The second waved a fist. "Scram, soldier. We got work to do." He set his hand on the drill.

The noise ate away Johnnie's eardrums. He couldn't hear what Mike was saying. The cop was making gestures at the men. They desisted.

"Now what?" the second guy demanded.

"Listen, Johnnie," Mike began. "Look at that hole. It isn't deep enough."

Johnnie looked. It wasn't a big hole; the surface wasn't cracked to a depth of more than a few inches. He said, "They can make it deeper."

"So you don't like our hole?" the first guy sighed. "I wish I was back at excavating. I'd show you a nice big hole. Besides kibitzers can't talk to you when you're excavating. If they do you can't hear them."

"Wait," Mike said to the hand on the drill. "Look, Johnnie, it isn't an excavation. The street department just breaks up the top layer. You couldn't hide anything there."

"Did you gents lose something?" Number Two asked.

"Yes," Johnnie answered promptly, and not so promptly "Well—no—yes—"

"Make up your mind."

"We might as well go back in," Mike urged. "Theo isn't here."

"I'm not so sure." Johnnie was belligerent. "They've been working a long time to make such a little hole."

"What do you want us to do, be unemployed by morning?" the first said. "Better take your pal away—say, you're a cop!"

"Off duty," Johnnie explained. He didn't want Mike to get in any trouble.

"Mike Costello." He introduced himself. "Sorry we bothered you. Come on, Johnnie."

"I'd like a better look at that hole," Johnnie persisted. He didn't continue. There was a little figure running toward them. It was Trudy.

"What are you two doing out here?" She was breathless. "Are you crazy?"

"Sure," the second man called out, loud and true.

"We're looking for Theo," Johnnie said with dignity.

"That's what I came to tell you. I've found him." She grabbed his hand. "Hurry!"

He didn't have time to think. He ran beside her back toward the house. Mike caught up with them.

"Where is he?"

"I'll show you."

They went inside again. She turned and closed the door softly. "Upstairs." They started fast. They were on the first step when she called, "Wait!" Both of them turned back.

She was standing against the door, far enough away to make a plunge impossible. There was a sweet smile on her face. In her hand was her gun. It pointed smack at them.

Six

"ROOKED AGAIN," Johnnie groaned.

"What's the big idea?" Mike doubled his fists.

"The big idea is that you're to put your hands out in front of you and climb up those stairs." She was little but there was nothing soft about her voice or the gun.

"You need some help, Trudy?" There was someone behind the chenille curtain now. Someone with a thick accent. It was Dorp.

"I found these two out in the street."

Anxiety popped his eyes. "They send no message?"

"I don't know. I don't think they had time."

"What were they doing?"

"Talking to those men fixing the street."

Dorp scowled. "Can you hold them here while I get together everyone? We must decide what now to do."

"You're darn right I can hold them," she stated. "One off beat and I'll get trigger finger."

Dorp waddled upstairs.

"Listen, Trudy." Johnnie tried to reason with her. "Mike's a cop. You can't shoot him."

"Keep your hands up," she commanded. "A dead cop's just as dead as a dead pigeon. In there."

They walked into her parlor.

Mike complained. "It's the last time I play Boy Scout to the Army. I should have been home in bed hours ago. With my shoes off."

Johnnie had no answer. He too could have had a good evening, chorus girls and fun. He certainly hadn't intended to sweat out a pass this way. He'd probably be too tired tomorrow for sight-seeing. And Bill and Hank would doubtless never speak to him even if he found them again.

Trudy eyed him reproachfully from the piano bench. "You've certainly messed things up, Johnnie Brown."

"Me?" He was indignant. He sputtered. "Me? Who was it dragged me upstairs tonight? Who was it handed me—"

She broke in loudly. "Keep quiet. I tried to get you to leave when you first barged in, remember? But no. You had to stick around. You deserve just what you get."

"Give me back my dog tags and I'll go right now."

"No, you won't," she slurred. "You haven't a chance of getting out until it's all over. And you'd better stop trying." She circled past them, the gun steady as a Texas Sheriff's. "You might tell me one thing. Did you send a message?"

"I wouldn't tell you the right time." Johnnie was glum. He and Mike should have called the police before looking at that hole in the street. He and Mike should never have followed Trudy back in here. He and Mike should have their respective heads examined.

176

"If you did," her smile was too sweet, "I'd advise you to lie about it when the others came down. They wouldn't like it."

"Wouldn't like what?" That was Rupe's voice behind them. "What gives now, Trudy? Why the ack-ack?"

"These two were trying to skip," she stated.

"How stupid. Hold it steady, baby mine."

Johnnie couldn't see what was happening. He heard Mike's shout, "Hey, you can't do that!" and Trudy's warning, "Keep those hands up, copper."

Ruprecht pranced over to her. He was fondling Mike's revolver with admiration.

"He took it right out of my holster," Mike complained. "Unbuttoned my holster and took it right out."

"You know my motto about dead cops," Trudy warned.

"At ease." Rupe put his arm around Trudy. His free hand held Mike's gun. "I'll keep them covered for you."

"Judas," said Mike sadly.

"You boys can sit down," Rupe said. "Right there on the floor. It's safe, Trudy. Johnnie doesn't have a gun. I tried to borrow one from him earlier. I have Mike's. Go on, sit down, fellows."

It wasn't very comfortable but they sat down on the worn red carpet. Mike said to Johnnie's ear, "Who's on who's side here?"

"Don't mutter," Rupe warned.

He repeated aloud, "Who's on who's side here?"

"I wish I knew," Trudy breathed.

Magda and Janssen came down together. Janssen's mouth was too red. That indelible stuff was hard to rub off quick. Mike glared at him. Magda's green eyes opened wide. "Why are they sitting there?"

"We're having a picnic, darling," Rupe drawled. "Johnnie and Mike arrived early."

"I'm not," Mike glowered.

Ferenz called out, "What does Dorp want now? He told us to come here." He stopped when he saw the picnickers, walked all around them cautiously. His mouth pursed out superciliously as he moved away.

Ottomkopf was next. He glared at the two prisoners. "What now have these spies did?"

"Who's a spy?" Johnnie demanded. "Don't answer, let me. You're a spy."

"Oh hush!" Ferenz was petulant.

Dorp dived through the curtains at last. "Are we all here? We must leave at once. These men—"

"Where's Rudolph?" Johnnie shouted suddenly. He scrambled up then gun or no gun.

Everyone looked at everyone else. All anyone saw was a frightened face. Ruprecht's voice threatened, "Where is Rudolph?"

Ottomkopf turned on Janssen. He thundered, "Where is Rudolph?"

Mike said with evident pleasure, "He started with Trudy."

"I turned him over to Janssen," she said quickly.

Janssen quavered, "I don't know. He told me he wanted to take a bath."

"He took one bath!" Dorp roared.

"He told me he didn't want to look for papers. He wanted a bath. I was outside his door. Then Magda came along and asked me to hunt with her. I—I—"

"Good hunting?" Mike asked with malice.

Janssen turned bricky.

"Mike," Ruprecht ordered, "You go stand guard at the front door. Don't let anyone in or out."

Mike lolled on the floor. "So you want to play with me now?"

"Don't be difficult," Rupe said. "Johnnie and I have to search the house. We don't want the murderer escaping while we search."

Mike clambered up reluctantly. "I'm not doing any guarding in this house without my gun."

"Sorry." Rupe handed it back to him just like that. Mike looked amazed. He took it as if there were a trick. "I'll use Trudy's."

Mike stuck the gun away. "How about the back door?"

"There's only the front staircase. Guard it."

"O.K." Mike turned to glare at the room. "Don't anybody be coming around with excuses. It won't do you no good."

"Come on, Johnnie," Rupe said. "Give me your gun, Trudy."

"I'm going with you, Rupe." She moved to his side.

"Give me your gun anyway."

"What about us?" Dorp ventured. "What do we do?"

"I don't care what you vultures do. Only I advise you to keep your eyes on each other." He eyed them singly. "I don't know who got rid of Rudolph. I only know who didn't. Johnnie and Mike didn't because they were outdoors. Trudy didn't. She was following them. And I know I didn't. That leaves the rest of you."

"Dear, what are you saying?" Ferenz' little eyes were pained.

"He's nuts," Magda shrugged. "He always was." She dug her hands into the pockets of her black velvet jacket. "I know what I'm going to do. Stay right here. I'm tired of searching this damn house. And if anyone has any ideas of making me disappear, I warn them to watch out." She flipped out her gun. "I know how to shoot."

"I'll be with you, Magda." Janssen licked his lips.

"Let's get going, Rupe," Johnnie said disgusted. Some girl friend. Didn't matter to her that Rudolph had probably been killed. Just as long as there was another guy handy.

Trudy trailed Johnnie and Rupe. Johnnie didn't like her behind him. Not with that habit she had of sticking a gun in a guy's backside.

He scowled his face at her. "What was the idea of holding me and Mike up with your gun? Like we were the enemy."

"Didn't you see Dorp watching us? Besides—" She shoved past him to Rupe's side. "Besides no matter how much I love you, Johnnie, I can't have you and your copper monkey-wrenching my plans. Not this late in the day. Guardroom, Rupe?"

"Yes." He headed toward Theo's room.

"Hadn't we ought to just look in his bathroom first?" Johnnie suggested.

"You don't think he's there, do you?" Rupe's face was grim. "Well, go on and look. I'm betting on the attic. If you find him, yell."

Trudy hesitated. "You don't expect to find him, do you?"

"Not alive." Rupe's mouth was a bitter line. "But I'll find him. And I'll find who did it." He halted. "You still don't have a gun, do you, Johnnie?"

Johnnie showed his muscle. "I don't need one." He didn't. He still had the bomb. He watched the two go into Theo's room, close the door. He himself headed for Rudolph's. He wasn't afraid to go in, but he was almost afraid to turn on the light. He'd seen one dead man in here tonight. It wasn't that ha'nts scared him but he didn't like the idea of finding corpses.

He closed his eyes before he switched the light. He opened them slowly as possible. The room was empty. He stood for a moment breathing again. No one on the floor. No one under the bed. No one in the closet. He went over to the bathroom door. He knocked. He knocked three times, each time louder. Finally he opened the door a teensy crack. He closed his eyes before he did it. Drowning in a bath tub wouldn't be something he wanted to remember. The bathroom was empty. There was one dampish towel hung over the tub. That would be the first bath. Rudolph hadn't taken a second. Not even a yardbird from Arkansas would use the same bath towel twice, not with a pole full of big clean ones at hand. Rudolph had not taken a second bath. That was an excuse to give Janssen the slip. It hit Johnnie like a ton of bricks. That closet wasn't just empty of dead bodies: it was empty. No coat and hat. The suitcase gone. The brief case gone. Rudolph had got away!

Johnnie ran to the window on the fire escape. He

pushed it up, leaned out. That was dopey. Rudolph would have left a long time ago whether he went by window or door. He wouldn't be hanging around waiting to be discovered. There wasn't any doubt in Johnnie's mind that Rudolph had skipped. Not when it was this easy. Rudolph didn't have the chin of a thinker but it wouldn't take much brain power for him to figure he was safer out of this house than in it. He, Johnnie, didn't claim to be any Eisenhower but he knew he'd be safer out of here. And, this was his chance.

He leaned out the window. Somewhere below that watchman might be prowling but he wouldn't be hard to handle. Johnnie hesitated. He didn't hesitate long. He drew back, closed the window. He couldn't skip without Mike. He'd brought the copper into this: he couldn't rat out. Not and leave Mike to fight off this bunch singlehanded. Besides if he walked out now he never would know how it turned out. And he couldn't leave without his dog tags. He was in to the finish. The finish was going to be soon. As soon as he reported that Rudolph had flown the coop.

He wasn't going to hurry with that information. Give a guy an outside chance to get clear. He, Johnnie, might as well put up his feet and have a smoke until Rupe and Trudy came back downstairs. He plumped the pillows behind his head on the old-fashioned mahogany four poster, stretched his feet out on the blue and white tufted spread. He lit a cigarette. This was solid comfort. This was what he'd been waiting for. He took a quick one at his watch. No wonder bed felt good. Four-thirty A.M.! He'd have to remember to keep his eyes open in this rest period. A catnap might turn into a real pounding of the ear and he'd miss what was going to happen. He wished he had a bottle of Rupe's champagne. That would wake him up. Or he wished he had Trudy around. He wouldn't feel like sleeping if she were here. He blew a whole chain of rings—pretty good ones, too—and thought about Trudy. Bill and Hank wouldn't believe he'd spent the evening with a blonde babe, cute as Sonja Henie, even if he could describe her to them. Nobody would.

He turned over and buried his ear in the pillow. He'd like to stay right here. Only you'd think they would furnish a mattress without lumps for Crown Princess Ermintrude of Rudamia. Maybe she knew how to avoid the bumps. Maybe . . .

Johnnie slid off the bed but fast. He shoved his hand under the blankets about where that hump had been. He drew out what his hand closed on.

Now he had a gun too. A gun with a silencer. The murderer hadn't taken much pains to hide it. Maybe he'd hoped Rudolph would find it, put his fingerprints on it. Johnnie's mouth turned wry. Big stupe, Johnnie. He'd done it all right. Now when he turned it over to the police, they'd have their murderer easy. One Pfc. John Brown. He shoved it in his pocket and he flopped down again on the bed. Hank had been right. It wasn't safe for him and Bill to let Johnnie go off alone.

He leaned up on his elbow suddenly. Somebody outside was turning the knob of the door. Johnnie lay still. He wasn't relaxed; he could have jumped and hit that door before it opened. But he wanted to see who it was. Maybe the murderer was coming back for his gun. Neither Trudy nor Rupe would be pussy-footing.

The door opened one small crack and then it started closing again. Johnnie sang out quick, "Come on in." He didn't want to have to get up and chase the intruder. His invitation worked. The door opened and Ferenz bounced through.

The big man closed the door behind him, looked around and pursed up his lips. "What are you doing?" he asked petulantly.

"Just resting," Johnnie said.

"You've found Rudolph?"

"Uh uh." He blew out a real thick ring. "He's gone."

"Gone?" Ferenz nearly screamed it. But softly. "Gone?"

"Uh huh." He didn't like fat pants with the squeaky voice.

"Where?"

"I don't know."

"Have you looked?"

"I don't have to look any more. His coat's gone. His hat's gone. Also his bags. He's gone all right."

Ferenz's face drooped down over his chins.

"There's a fire escape outside the window."

"You don't have to tell me! I own this house." But he billowed over, opened the window and peered out. "He took everything?"

"Yeah."

"The traitor. All that money. Sixty-five thousand dollars I put up to send him back to Rudamia."

"It wasn't sixty-five thousand. It was seven thousand."

"Sixty-five thousand, I tell you." Ferenz turned a face like a tomato. An over-ripe one. "I know how much money I have spent on him, don't I? And how does he repay? By running to Washington to get me in bad with the government!" He stuck out his head again, withdrew it, banged down the window and swirled on Johnnie. "You knew he'd gone! And you lay here resting!"

Johnnie rolled off the bed, keeping it between them and the big fellow. Ferenz looked mad enough to froth. "I was waiting for Trudy and Rupe to come back." Johnnie opened his eyes full after he'd said that. It hadn't occurred to him before. Maybe he'd been snipe-hunting, he and Mike. Maybe those two weren't coming back. He made for the door.

Ferenz screamed, "Where are you going?"

He didn't bother to answer. Ferenz was puffing on his heels. Johnnie whirred into Theo's room, pushed aside the secret closet and bellowed up into the dimness, "Rupe, Trudy, get down here. Double time." Silence alone answered him. He called again, "Trudy, Rupe!" There was no answer.

He plunged past Ferenz, almost knocking him down as he tore by him and down the stairs to the parlor. He swooped open the chenille curtains.

No one was in the room. No one at all.

2.

Ferenz came to a halt behind him. He was winded. He gasped, "Are you crazy?"

"Look." Johnnie pointed to the obvious. "They've all skipped. Not just Rupe and Trudy. All of them." He swung suddenly. "Mike!"

Crash-bang answered him. He shoved Ferenz, stepped out into the hall. Mike was on the floor. So was the chair. "I wasn't asleep," Mike denied. "I was sabotaged."

"They're gone!" Johnnie shouted.

Ferenz spoke wearily. "Don't be an ass. They're upstairs for a bite to eat. Loathsome food. Cold sandwiches."

Johnnie didn't look at Mike. He stubbed up the stairs after Ferenz. He'd forgotten the lure of food.

They were stuffing placidly, Magda, Janssen, Ottomkopf, Dorp. They weren't in the least interested in Johnnie's appearance in the doorway. Magda spoke through a sandwich. "Where was he?"

"He wasn't." Ruprecht and Trudy couldn't have helped but heard his roar. No matter how much wooing was going on. If they'd been up there.

Ferenz sat down at the head of the table. "A cup of coffee, please dear. Rudolph has left us."

Janssen's mouth alone dropped open. "You mean—like Theo?"

"I don't mean anything of the sort," Ferenz snapped. "I mean bag and baggage." He pushed the cup away. "With what do you adulterate your coffee, Herr Dorp, soybeans? I cannot endure bad coffee. Mine I fly in once a week from South America. Doubtless Rudolph is even now en route to Washington, to the government-in-exile. There is no possible way to stop him."

"And why not?" Ottomkopf demanded.

"My dear, do you suggest that one of us attempt abducting him from the Pennsylvania Station or from the airport? There are laws in this country." He flung down the cake he was absent-mindedly nibbling. "I abhor pink icing!" He brushed off his fingers. "I too am leaving. I told you I did not wish to appear in this. You have in-

volved me against my will. Pray do not bother me again
—any of you."

Magda choked on crumbs. "What about the missing
papers?"

"I know nothing of them. Doubtless one of you do. If
they are ever found, I suggest sending them to Rudolph,
in internment. With my compliments." He pushed up.
"Good night."

Dorp jumped to face him. "I do not think you should
leave us like this."

"Do I care what you think?" He drew himself up to
six foot two inches of floppy dignity. "I am Ferenz
Lessering."

"What's up now?" Ruprecht asked mildly.

Johnnie could have cheered. Good old Rupe! He
hadn't ratted. Neither had Trudy. She was right behind
him, pink and pretty and curious.

"Rudolph's skipped," Johnnie explained.

"Skipped? What do you mean?"

Ferenz said, "Just what he says. Rudolph has gone.
Coat, hat, luggage—gone." His chest began to heave.
"All my money gone. Gone with one who sneaks away
to tell the F.B.I. what I have done for him."

Ruprecht began to laugh. Trudy looked at him and
she began to laugh too.

"I wouldn't have thought he had enough guts," Rupe
chortled. "Good old Rudo. I'll buy him a drink when
he gets out of internment." He became straight-faced.
"Maybe he didn't like your plans." He looked at each
one of them in turn.

"What do you mean?" Ferenz asked haughtily.

"Maybe he figured he'd rather be a live duck under suspicion than a dead one under the plans."

Ferenz shook his head. "There was the risk, Ruprecht, always the risk in king-making. But a throne is worth the gamble. And Dorp had it directly from Europe—"

"How do you know?" Ruprecht demanded. "Anybody could tell you anything so long as you agreed with it. How do you know what Dorp dreamed up?"

"You are speaking of me?" Dorp squawked.

Johnnie liked this.

"Yeah, you. Why wouldn't you dream them pretty when you'd found a sucker who didn't care what he put out for as long as he could play Metternich. But murder's a different story."

"So are Nazis," Johnnie allowed.

Magda commanded, "Quiet!"

It was the first time she'd pulled that in hours. Johnnie was so surprised he turned and looked at her. She wasn't paying any attention to him though. She'd said it automatically. She was watching Ferenz. Johnnie was thankful he wasn't Ferenz. Those green eyes were more like the eyes of a rattler than of a glamour girl. If he hadn't been on the wrong side of the table, Johnnie would have made a dive for her gun pocket. He didn't think she was safe having it at the moment.

Ferenz didn't seem worried though. He was merely tired of it all. He droned, "I am leaving here, Ruprecht. Find out what you can, dear, and let me know. I am writing this project off as a bad debt. Perhaps the Rudamian *Republic* will some day reimburse me."

"What makes you think you're leaving?" Magda asked

softly. "You're in this too, Furry. Don't think you're not. If the rest of us are investigated, we're not going to pretend we dug up the money out of Fort Knox to send Rudolph back to Rudamia."

"I do not intend to figure in this, Magda." Ferenz' voice rose. "Whatever lies you choose to tell about me, my lawyers and I shall refute with ease."

He walked to the door. Ruprecht still blocked it. Magda's hand was in her pocket. Dorp spoke. "Let him go." It was an order.

Ruprecht stepped aside. Now Trudy barred the way. Ferenz could squash Trudy like she was a crocus. He didn't. She raised her big blue eyes to him. "Don't you want to help us find Theo? And whoever murdered him?"

"Theo is of no possible interest to me," Ferenz answered loftily. "I am leaving here at once. I would advise the rest of you to do the same as quickly as possible. Once Rudolph reaches the government-in-exile, I fear the F.B.I. will be headed this way. Even if they do not come, I am supporting this house no longer. You have bungled. All of you. Good night." He pushed her aside.

Dorp repeated, "Let him go."

Trudy grinned. "He won't get far. Mike's got integrity."

Dorp's fat face split. "I too remembered Mike."

Even Ottomkopf simulated their giggles.

Dorp brushed the crumbs off his vest and belched. "I do not believe Mr. Lessering should be allowed to leave without us." He trotted into the throne room. The others followed. "Phew," he said. "Phew." His nose wrinkled. "This room. It smells." He pulled the red curtains away from the front windows, flung the windows wide.

"Is this wise?" Ottomkopf asked dubiously.

"Why not? It is almost daylight. The prize has vanished. The rest of us too must vanish."

From below there were voices. The injured bleat was Ferenz. The bluster was Mike.

Magda smiled. "You think we should prepare to leave with Ferenz?"

"I believe this would be the wise move," Dorp stated.

From below there rose the plaint, "Ruprecht, this fellow refuses to allow me to depart."

Mike's voice climbed over it. "I got my orders, Bub."

Johnnie slid along to the banisters, leaned over. It was just like it sounded. The big Lessering stood at bay at the foot of the stairs, trembling with rage. Mike was on both feet by the door, twirling his service revolver and looking pleased as Punch. Johnnie cheered, "At-a-boy!"

"Ruprecht!" Ferenz wailed.

Ruprecht hadn't come out of the throne room yet. The others had, all but Trudy. They were bustling around, upstairs, in rooms, out of rooms. All the while Ferenz kept howling for Ruprecht. Johnnie felt a nudge on his arm. It was Trudy squeezing up beside him. That felt good. It would have felt better if Rupe hadn't come along pushing on the other side of her. She didn't honey up to him though. She urged, "Go on, Rupe."

"And miss the fun? Not yet. Don't worry about me."

Mike was finally making himself heard above the din.

He spoke to the point. "Aw, shut up before I let you have it."

By that time Dorp and Ottomkopf were hurrying down the stairs, bowlered and coated. After them came Janssen, his uniform enveloped by the dark coat again, and Magda, a polo coat over her yellow slacks. At the same moment the pounding at the front door broke through the racket.

Johnnie felt relieved. Some way Mike had got word through to headquarters. If it weren't the police, it must be the Marines. This was the spot for them.

Mike pointed a steady gun to the crowd on the staircase. "Stay right where you are," he said.

Johnnie whispered to Trudy. "Might as well see the show in comfort." He took her by the hand and hurried her to the top step. "Box seats," he offered. They sat down. The only trouble was that Rupe followed, sitting down on the other side of Trudy.

"You are no longer to guard," Dorp was announcing to Mike but he didn't attempt to move from the lower step.

"The hell I'm not," Mike told him. The door pounding wasn't quieting down any. Mike shouted to it, "Keep your shirt on." He backed nearer to the noise while warning the tableau, "One of you make a false move and you'll see if I'm still on guard." He put his hand on the knob, opened the door without turning. "Come in and join the party. Keep quiet and watch this gun." He kept the shooting iron and eyes pointed steady forward.

Johnnie lifted up from the step but Trudy pulled him down. "Wait," she ordered. She was watching the door.

The new entrants weren't policeman. They were the two street department men with the hats pulled over their eyes. Johnnie had known they were phonies. Real street department workers wouldn't be coming in here. He would have warned Mike but it happened too fast. Before he could yell, one of them had lunged, quietly knocked the revolver out of Mike's hand. The gun bumped across the floor. Dorp picked it up, scurried to a stand in front of the chenille curtains where he covered not only the bunch on the stairs but the three by the door. The only ones he didn't cover were Johnnie and Trudy and Rupe on the top step. He didn't know they were there.

Mike's fist had shot out the minute he was attacked. The workman's chum had closed in. You couldn't see what was what by now.

"Stop that horseplay," Dorp commanded once he was set. "Stand where you are."

Mike and the wrestling team moved apart. One workman had an incipient shiner. The other was wiping his nose. Mike brushed at his sleeves.

"Now I have something to say," Dorp announced. "Thank you, Joe."

"Wasn't nothing," Joe said. He picked up his hat, pulled it over one eye like before.

Johnnie whispered, "Why can't I go down the back way and sneak up on Dorp from behind?"

"No back stairs," Trudy whispered. "Wait." She had her eyes fixed on the door again.

"May we leave now?" Ferenz was haughty.

"Not yet," said Dorp. "Not until I know who killed Theo."

"Does it matter?" Ferenz wearily examined his nails.

"He was a traitor," Ottomkopf growled. "He deserved to die. Let us go."

"He did not deserve to die," Dorp said slowly. "He was a poor weak fool, yes. A tool, yes. But I did not intend he should die. I should myself have protected him had I known he was to die. I did not know. Now I shall find out who it was killed him."

"You're being frightfully silly, Dorp." Ferenz was impatient. "We can confer at a safer place than this. Even now Rudolph may be in Washington, may have set on us the F. B. I."

Dorp laughed, a noisy jiggling laugh. "The F. B. I. is not coming up from Washington to investigate us. This need not worry your head."

Rupe's jaw was set. He leaned forward. Trudy's hand went swiftly to his arm. She still watched the door with puzzled anxiety.

"What do you mean?" Ferenz' whisper was shrill.

Magda cried, "What do you mean? You didn't—Rudolph isn't—dead?"

Dorp laughed louder. When he stopped the silence was thick as his accent. He spoke into it. "I hope he is not dead. If he is someone will be sorry, very sorry."

The silence was awkward. Ferenz began, not so sure of himself now, "I cannot remain here longer."

Dorp moved the gun forward. "But you will," he said softly. "Or I shall be forced to shoot this gun at you."

"I scarcely knew this Theo."

"I didn't know him at all," Ottomkopf spoke up.

"No. But it was not Theo who was meant to die. It

was Theo who died but it was meant to be Rudolph. And there were many who wish Rudolph to die."

"You can't include me!" Magda exclaimed.

"Indeed yes, Magda. If Rudolph dies, who is king? Ruprecht, yes. And much better you should be his queen, no?"

Trudy made an ugly face.

"I wasn't betrothed to Ruprecht."

"It is the royal custom," Dorp smiled, "that if a betrothal is made publicly—as it was tonight—the lady must be taken over by the new king. Ruprecht could do nothing but marry you."

"I could abdicate," Ruprecht muttered.

Ottomkopf said, "That is quite true, Herr Dorp. She killed Theo."

"I did not!" Magda shouted. "What about you? You never could get along with Rudolph."

"It appears to me," Ferenz stated, "that Ruprecht had the most to gain by Rudolph's death."

Ruprecht spoke again under his breath. "My pal."

"I certainly have nothing to gain," Ferenz continued. "If Rudolph had been killed tonight, I should have lost a goodly sum of money, the cost of bringing him from Mexico, the ticket on the Clipper, the expenses involved—"

"Maybe," Dorp agreed. "Maybe not. There is a good price on Rudolph's head. Put there by the Nazis who now hold Rudamia. The same price is on Ruprecht's head. That is why the F. B. I. watch so closely on him, I believe. The Nazis would eliminate the heirs to the Rudamian throne. Believing this would save them a revolution."

"For someone who poses as a Rudamian patriot," Ferenz said meanly, "It seems to me you know a lot about Nazi affairs."

"Of certainty I do. It is because these things I know that I am able to help you plan Rudolph's return. I am an honest man. I do not like it that one of you is not honest. That one of you pretends only that he wishes Rudolph to return. I do not like it that he is brought here only to be killed. I particularly do not like it that one of you kills poor Theo by mistake."

Janssen spoke up suddenly. "Herr Dorp, there is one question you must answer. Why did you give that envelope to Theo? Everything starts from that point."

"I am asking the questions," Dorp reminded him coldly. "Remember that. Which of you killed Theo?"

Silence alone answered him.

"I could tell him," Johnnie muttered.

Trudy put her finger to her lips.

"If that is not to be answered by you, I do not anticipate the consequences. Not pleasureably for you. I and my men will—"

Trudy let out her breath. Someone had knocked on the front door. The knock was repeated.

"See who this is, Joe," Dorp frowned.

Joe opened the door. Whoever Trudy had been expecting, this wasn't it. Nor was it the Marines.

It was Rudolph.

3.

It was Rudolph, a Rudolph with a satisfied canary-filled expression on his vacant face and his long cigarette holder angled in his mouth. No one expected him. The lower stair delegation reared forward as one man. Ruprecht and Johnnie grabbed Trudy's arm just in time to keep her from tumbling on her head. Disappointment was fluctuating with amazement on her face. Dorp's mouth was wondrous. But he didn't forget to keep the gun pointed at his prisoners.

Magda recovered first. "Rudolph! Where have you been?"

"I was hungry," he said blandly.

"We had supper prepared."

He lifted supercilious eyebrows. "There was no chile. I told you I wanted some chile."

"But how did you get out?"

He frowned at her stupidity. "How do you think? On wings? I walked out the front door, of course. And I found a nice little restaurant, open all night, on the next street. Strange. The man who runs it is from Rudamia. Hans—"

"Your bags?" Dorp demanded. "What did you do with your bags?"

"Aren't they here? I told that guard to watch them." He was annoyed. "What are you doing with that gun, Dorp? I brought them down myself. It was almost time to go to the airport. I left them by the halltree there."

Johnnie peered through the banisters. They were there all right. Only everyone here, inspired by a dumb private from Texas, was so certain that Rudolph had flown the roost they hadn't bothered to look in the dark passageway.

Dorp too had glanced. "They are there. Please to join the others on the stairs, Rudolph."

"What for? Aren't we going to La Guardia field? Do you mean no one yet gave up the papers you were stewing about?"

"You haven't been to Washington?" Ferenz asked anxiously.

"How silly." Rudolph dropped ashes. "How could I get to Washington and back in less than an hour, Furry? I went to eat some chile. Hans didn't have chile but he had sauerbraten and some good beer. What about those papers?"

"They have not been recovered," Dorp said. "The important part of them is still missing. If you will now obey please and take your place on the stairs."

"I don't know why anyone would want to sit on the stairs. And I don't know why you're wasting time this way."

"I am not wasting time." Dorp's lip protruded. "I am finding the murderer of Theo."

"He probably killed himself," Rudolph offered. "From chagrin."

"With what? His fingernails?"

"All right, he didn't." Rudolph elbowed past Ferenz on the lower step, shook off Magda's fingers and continued climbing.

Dorp roared, "You are not to go upstairs."

Rudolph turned in annoyance. "I don't know why not. If Rupe can sit upstairs, why can't I?"

Trudy groaned.

Dorp lifted his eyes. "Sooo? So you are here. Even our soldier friend is yet with us. You will join the others down here if you please."

"The hell we will," Johnnie said pleasantly. He

shook off Trudy's fingers and rose up. His hand went into his pocket, came out with the cigar. He put it to his mouth. "See this? Know what it is? It's what you've been calling papers all night. It isn't papers."

"It's a cigar," Rudolph said.

"It isn't a cigar. It's a neat job. I'm in the Army. I know about these things." He put it closer to his teeth. "And I'm the guy who knows how to pull the pin. And if you don't drop that gun, I'll pull it."

"Blow us all up?" Mike shouted.

Johnnie felt very brave and patriotic at the moment. "Rather than let these Nazis loose, yes!" He apologized quickly, "Sorry, Mike. Okay, Dorp. One—two—"

Dorp let the gun fall. He didn't like doing it.

"Get it, Mike," Johnnie called. "And the rest of you hold still. One wiggle and—"

Mike had recovered the gun. With it in hand he waved the two workman into the lower stair group. He growled, "All right, Dorp. Get over."

Dorp said, "You are making a mistake. I work for the F. B. I."

"Oh yeah?" Johnnie could think of nothing more devastating to say at the moment.

"That is true, Private Johnnie Brown. Joe and Jorge here are members of the F. B. I. I help them. They help me. They have been waiting all evening outside to apprehend some of these people. Even now while I have talked, it was just that we must wait until the cars arrive to convey these enemy aliens to headquarters where questioning will be more successful."

Johnnie held the bomb handy. "Watch that door, Mike," he warned. "If any more of Dorp's F. B. I. gets here, let them have it. I guess you think I'd fall for anything, Pudgey, just because I'm from Texas. If those guys were really F. B. I. they wouldn't have jumped Mike."

"They don't know he's a cop. I don't know myself what he is. Anyone can borrow a uniform. He has behaved rather exceptional since he has arrived." He looked from Magda to Mike. Mike scuffed a toe. Dorp turned again to Johnnie. "Your motives are admirable, Private Brown, but you make a mistake. If I were not what I say I could have shot you when first you showed the bomb to me."

"And risk it exploding?" Ferenz squealed.

"That would not happen until the pin is pulled, or in due time is dissolved."

Johnnie sent it solid. "You know all about it, Herr Dorp."

"Yes, indeed," he said proudly. "I examined the envelope when first it came to me. I prised away the seals, saw what it contained."

"And didn't call the cops," Johnnie snapped.

"No. I have the evidence. That will not run away." He scowled. "So I think." His head nodded. "I do not wish the cops; the F. B. I. and myself will take care of matters when all the elements have come together. But I do not risk being asked to hand over the envelope prematurely. It is possible someone suspect I am not what I seem. It is possible that the envelope is taken from me, the envelope which will blow him up, and given to Rudolph; then him secreted away while I am at Mr. Lessering's. I do not wish Rudolph to be hurt. He is what you call the innocent bystander." He scowled ferociously. "It is others whom I and the Department of Justice wish to apprehend."

His shoulders shrugged. "I give the envelope to Theo—the misguided youth who plays with fire, an enemy patriot—no one will suspect he has it. He is too unimportant for that. If I am asked for it I will say it is not with me. We will all return to my house where my men watch outside. I will keep Rudolph safe while I bag the traitors."

"If you were going to bag them, why didn't you?" Johnnie demanded. "What have you been waiting for all night—Christmas?"

"Interruptions!" Dorp exploded. "Interruptions! First Rudolph must go to the party. Before my men arrive he must leave. When finally we manage to bring him back, the evidence is missing. Then Theo is killed. Comings and goings, comings and goings, but no evidence." He demanded, "And how did you get it?"

"Trudy hooked it out of Theo's pocket," Johnnie grinned. "She gave it to me for the same reason you gave it to Theo, no one would suspect me of having it."

She glared at him. "You told me there was nothing in it but the papers."

"There was, though." He grinned to his ears now. "I unsealed the seals just like Dorp and then I sealed it up again. Rudolph watched me." He scowled. "Only I kept the evidence on me. Wanted to make sure nobody got hurt. It didn't make any difference to me what happened to the goon but I didn't want the Clipper blown up. Nobody but a Nazi would think of anything as awful as blowing up a Clipper just to get rid of one guy. Only maybe the guy wasn't the important thing.

Maybe the whole deal was just to blow up the Clipper and whoever was on it this morning."

"That's smart figuring," Joe of the pulled down hat admitted. "Imagine the stink if an American Clipper exploded with important politicians aboard."

He talked as if he knew something. He didn't talk like a street worker at all. Johnnie squinted at what was visible of the face.

Trudy pulled his sleeve. "Johnnie."

Out of the side of his mouth, like a gangster, he shot, "Don't bother me. Can't you see I'm busy?"

"Johnnie," she clarioned. "Tell Mike to open that door and start blowing his police whistle. Tell him to keep blowing it until help comes." She called down, "Can you hold the gun and blow at the same time, Mike?"

"Watch me." He flung the door wide. Daylight was gray outside. Mike stepped into the opening, stood facing the staircase as he began to shrill.

Ruprecht sighed. "This calls for refreshments, Johnnie. We still have our bottles upstairs. I'll get them."

"Wait," Dorp cried. "Do not let him escape."

"He's going for our champagne." Johnnie shouted with what he hoped was sufficient frigidity above the din.

"You're in the groove." Rupe pounded his shoulder.

Trudy said ,"Eeow," and rubbed where he had passed her.

"Don't squeal. See you soon, baby mine. Here's your popgun. Be good or you won't share the rations."

A man had appeared in the doorway behind Mike.

He was just an ordinary homely guy in a dark suit with sleepy eyes. "What the hell are you doing here, Mike?" he demanded.

Mike said, "Didn't expect to draw you, Lefty."

Lefty came on into the room, looked tentatively at the haul. He didn't glance up the stairs until Trudy called, "Lefty, where have you been?"

His face was sour. "Where have I been? I been in that damn doorway across the street ever since seven o'clock last night. Ever since I talked to you in the basement."

The faces below weren't faces. They were big blanks.

"All ready to close in and what happens? You signal me, don't come."

"That was because Rudolph insisted on going out."

"Back you come. Signal stand by. I stand by. What happens? No signal."

"Ferenz was coming. I knew it wouldn't do any good to signal while he was here. He'd just get all his Washington bigwig friends to get the Nazis off."

"Why, Trudy." Ferenz was hurt.

"I wanted to get rid of him first. But then things got too bad. Rudolph disappeared. And I signaled you and you didn't come and didn't come—"

"I fell asleep," Lefty admitted glumly. "Even a police lieutenant gets sleepy after a fifty-two hour shift." He took a more thorough dig at the assemblage. "Okay. Do we run them all in?" His face brightened. "Hi there, Joe. Jorge. You guys on business?"

Dorp was giggling. "It is very funny. I have my men waiting. And you too, Trudy. A double guard." He shook his finger. "I always knew you were a good girl in the heart."

Johnnie said, "They say they're F. B. I.'s."

"Who are you?" Lefty demanded. "Sure they're F. B. I.'s."

Johnnie's grip on the bomb weakened. "Dorp too?" Lefty couldn't be a phony; Mike knew him.

Lefty said, "How do, Professor Dorp. Didn't see you at first in the crowd."

Johnnie repeated wanly, "Is Dorp F. B. I. too?" He hoped Ruprecht would get back fast with the champagne. He needed it.

"I am a military secret," Dorp stated proudly.

"That's about right," Lefty agreed. "Well, I guess we aren't needed here, Mike. Not with the Feds on the job."

Johnnie still couldn't trust. He didn't want Mike to leave. He shouted quick, "Tell him about the murder."

"Yeah, murder," Mike remembered. "Only no body." He scratched his head. "We never got to finish looking, Johnnie. Say, there's some cars stopping out front."

"Our fellows," Joe nodded.

"How about asking them to wait," Lefty requested. "Murder. I'd like a crack at this bunch before you take them in. Maybe if I solve a murder I'll get boosted to Inspector."

"Mike's done all the work," Johnnie yelled. "You got to make him a lieutenant or I won't tell you who did it."

Mike spoke placatingly. "He's my friend, Lefty. You know who did it, Johnnie?"

"I know how to find out," he said. "Only first I want to know who put the bomb in that letter."

"Bomb!" Lefty popped. "Mike, call the bomb squad quick."

Dorp bowed. "If you will give it to me, Private Brown. Any minute now it might explode. The Clipper left one hour ago, you know."

Rudolph sprang to life. "Why am I not on it?"

Magda sighed from her toes. "For God's sake."

"We got a better idea for you," Joe told him.

Dorp said, "If you will but carefully pass to me the bomb, Private Brown."

"I don't know." Johnnie examined it cautiously. He still wasn't certain about Dorp.

"You'd better give it to him, Johnnie," Trudy urged.

"Give it to him," Janssen insisted.

Ferenz pouted. "Make him give it to you, Dorp."

"We will all be blown up," Ottomkopf said hoarsely.

Jorge bounded up the steps. "I'll take care of it, soldier." He grabbed it, bounded down again and out the door.

Everyone but Johnnie sighed relief. He said. "Now I got nothing to protect myself with." He did have. The murderer's gun.

"I'll protect you," Mike promised. "Now, who killed Theo?"

Johnnie sat down on the top step. Rupe was sure taking his time. "First let's find out who fixed the bomb." The sea of faces was annoyed with him. "Well, why not? I got to be back in camp in the morning. I want to know what this is all about. You know it'll be censored out of the newspapers. How can I fight a war if I got to be worrying about this thing for the duration? Besides the same person did both. Both were jobs to kill Rudolph."

Rudolph said simply, "I wish I'd stayed in Mexico."

"So do I," Magda sighed.

Trudy said, "If I'd learned sooner what was up, I'd have seen that you stayed there, Rudolph."

"Traitor," said Magda.

"Are you admitting you knew it was a Nazi plot?" Trudy demanded.

The F. B. I. and New York's finest both moved in closer.

"Don't talk that way to her." Janssen's arm went around Magda's shoulders.

Rudolph squealed, "Take your hands off my betrothed."

Janssen ignored him.

Dorp spoke calmly. "It was Magda gave me that envelope."

Her voice rose swiftly. "Ottomkopf gave it to me."

Ottomkopf was apoplectic. "You cannot accuse me. I did not open the envelope. I did not know what I carried when I came to this house. Ferenz Lessering asked me to bring it to Dorp. Magda took it from me here."

"Yes," Ferenz nodded. "Yes, I gave it to Ottomkopf to carry. Janssen had brought it to me. He had an important guard meeting. He could not convey it to Herr Dorp."

Janssen said quickly, "I picked it up for Herr Dorp at our Brooklyn headquarters."

"Ring around the rosy," Trudy sang.

Magda spoke up nastily. "Don't forget Trudy handled it."

"That does not work." Dorp shook his head. "I had opened it before she took it."

"Perhaps," Magda agreed. "But you did not open it at once. You put it on the desk in your room while you conferred with Ottomkopf."

"How do you know?" Trudy asked. "You can't black-wash me, wench. If I'd filched it then I wouldn't have had to pick Theo's pocket tonight."

"Last night," Johnnie yawned.

"And I wouldn't have had Lefty in a drafty areaway all night if I was in on it."

Dorp said briskly, "This is no good. We take them to headquarters. It is too bad for Private Brown's curiosity"—he shrugged—"but we can waste no more time."

"Wait a minute," Lefty demanded. "What about that murder?" He squinted up at Johnnie. "If you want Mike to solve it, you'd better spill."

"Oh that," Johnnie said. "First get their guns." He didn't want the murderer taking a pot shot at him before he named names.

"Pass 'em out," Lefty barked. "Anybody got identifying tags to mark them with?"

Jorge announced, "Always prepared." He fished in his pocket.

"The Marines!" Johnnie cried joyously.

Magda's was first. Janssen had his in the pocket where his hand had rested in the car. Hours ago. Yesterday. From Ottomkopf, Mike produced a nasty Luger.

"I have none," Rudolph said sweetly.

"Nor have I," Ferenz growled. "I am not in the habit of carrying a gun."

"You too, Trudy," Johnnie urged.

"All right, Benedict Arnold." She handed it down to the F. B. I. man.

"Now listen," Johnnie began. This was the difficult part. "I have the murderer's gun." He pulled it from his pocket. "I found it where he'd hidden it. In Rudolph's bed."

"Trudy's bed," Rudolph prompted.

"It's got my fingerprints all over it. So I found it." He defied them. "Even if you can't find the murderer's fingerprints underneath you can prove I didn't do it."

Ferenz spoke up. "I knew all along this man was dangerous. Arrest him, officer."

"You can prove it easy," Johnnie persisted. "You know how?"

"Yeah," Lefty nodded. "The paraffin test for hands."

Everyone turned the palms of his hands up. Everyone automatically examined those of his neighbor.

"I shall protest to my government-in-exile," Rudolph proclaimed.

Johnnie cleared his throat preparatory to an important speech. "The murderer," he said solemnly, "is Ferenz Lessering."

Seven

"What!" Ferenz rocked to his toes. He was wrapped in disdain. "You are being absolutely absurd. I shall speak to my friend J. Edgar Hoover about this. I shall speak to Attorney-General Biddle. I shall speak—"

"Speak to everybody," Johnnie cried blissfully. "Speak to Mayor La Guardia and Mr. Hopkins and Eleanor Roosevelt and Senator Knox and General Mac-Arthur and my top sergeant—" He grinned. "They won't speak to you."

"Ferenz Lessering." Lefty was dubious.

"I suspected him all along," Johnnie said sagely. "Any guy that has as much food stored away as Mr. Lessering couldn't be any good. He smuggles coffee too. He said so tonight."

"I said no such thing!" Ferenz denied. "I am a coffee importer."

"Tell that to the Marines," Johnnie advised. "But tonight when he came sneaking up to Rudolph's room to get the gun he'd hidden in the bed, then I knew."

"This man is insane!" Ferenz quivered. "I don't believe he's a soldier at all."

"I am too!" Johnnie retorted. "I'll show you my dog tags." He turned to Trudy. "Give me my dog tags."

Wordless she dug them out of her pocket.

He dangled them aloft. "See?" Everyone saw. "He thought he was killing Rudolph but he killed Theo by mistake—"

"Why would I kill Rudolph?" Ferenz wept. "Already he has cost me a small fortune."

Dorp patted his fat vest. "I believe Johnnie is right. I eliminate. Who will gain by Rudolph's death? Not I. Not even in my role as the loyal German-Rudamian who trains the young patriots. If Rudolph dies there are no patriots to train. Herr Ottomkopf? If he wishes

Rudolph to die it is very simple to kill him in Mexico. A bit of poison in the chile. Who could taste it?" He sputtered. "Who could taste anything in that. Ruprecht? Where is Ruprecht?"

"He's icing the champagne," Trudy said.

"Very well. He does not wish to be king."

"So he says," Ferenz put in.

"He does not. I know. Did not Herr Ottomkopf and myself try to persuade him to be king when first you broached the idea of kingmaking? Rudolph would be persuaded to abdicate."

"I would not!" Rudolph squealed.

"For good pay, yes, you would. Ruprecht would make the better king, says Herr Ottomkopf. But Ruprecht refuses. Hence he would not kill his brother to receive what he could have without the trouble. Magda wishes to be queen. She prefers Ruprecht but a bird in the hand is better eating." Dorp's voice perked up. "Who is it insists Rudolph come here to fly to South America? Who? It is Ferenz Lessering. It is his price for redeeming the Rudamian ruby for Magda. The ruby which Herr Ottomkopf has pawned. Only if she insists that Rudolph come here to sign the marriage papers. Why would Ferenz Lessering wish Rudolph here but to send him to his death? Are there not good airports in Mexico City?"

"I'll sue you for every cent you own!" Lessering screamed.

"You deny it? Ah, but there is a reason behind it. You are a man of high finance, Mr. Lessering. You will spend money to make money, yes? But you will not throw it away. Already you have spent more than you can afford on Rudolph. And Rudolph is such poor pay, always. But if Rudolph is dead, Ruprecht will be king. You and Ruprecht are such good friends, no? For months you have been together making these plans—"

"I demand the best lawyers," Lessering bellowed. "Let me out of here. My lawyers will answer you."

"You're going out, Bub. Don't worry about that." Joe stepped up to him.

"Feet first if you don't pipe down," Jorge added.

He took one look at them, huffed, "If you refuse to allow me to pass, I shall go telephone my lawyers. At once." He started up the stairs two at a time. Johnnie didn't hesitate. He ducked the outswung arm, caught Ferenz by a thumb and swung him up over his shoulder.

"Look!" he crowed. "Commando stuff."

He started with him back down the stairs. Ferenz was a cream puff. But two hundred ninety pounds of cream puff was just that. And Ferenz wasn't cooperating. He wiggled. Johnnie lost his footing halfway down. He fell against the banisters. They couldn't take it. He released Ferenz as they hurtled through space. From all the screaming and shouting, he thought he must have broken his head right open. He hadn't. Ferenz had cushioned his fall. It was like landing on a sofa. "Give a guy air," he complained to the crowd.

Ferenz wasn't hurt much either. He wouldn't have been yowling so loud if he had been. Yowling, "Get off of me, you lout. I'll see my lawyers."

Johnnie crawled off. And his eyes opened wide. "Theo!" he breathed. That was Theo propped in the corner, in the darkest far corner.

Rudolph whispered, "I thought it was a guard. I told him to watch my bags."

"It is Theo Kraken. Dead," said a hoarse voice.

Everyone looked up and around at the tall man with the scar splitting his face. Hans was peering over the huddle of heads.

"Did you say Kraken?" Rudolph shivered.

He nodded solemnly. "Yes. The young brother of Ipomio Kraken. I did not know he was in New York. It was he who drew the short straw—my cousin told me this—at the last meeting of the Terrorists before the war. It was he who was to kill His Highness, Prince Rudolph."

Janssen's voice shook. "And it was Theo who gave me the bomb."

Rudolph spoke up brightly. "Then I had a right to kill him. It was in self-defense."

Johnnie got to his feet. "Say that slow, brother."

"You killed him?" Lefty yelled.

"In self-defense," said Rudolph proudly. "I came out of my bath as he was trying to escape through the window. I thought it was my suitcase he carried. With all that money in it." He beamed. "Instead he was trying to escape before he was arrested for killing me. I killed him in self-defense."

"I shall get you the best lawyers, dear," Ferenz spat.

Rudolph turned in accusation on Dorp. "You told me you'd get rid of the body."

Dorp sighed. "The boys promised they would. They must have been afraid they'd miss the last train home. They are not well disciplined, I fear." He winked at Joe and Jorge. "I thought it best we hide the body for a little until more important things were taken care of."

"More important things?" Lefty scratched his head hard.

"Yes." Dorp's mouth set. "Yes. More important that we apprehend Herr Ottomkopf. The villain!"

"You speak of me?" Ottomkopf spluttered.

"Yes," said Dorp. "There he is, Joe, Jorge. The man who smuggled the Rudamian jewels into this country. Smuggled them encased in particularly evil-smelling cheese. You remember the cheese? This is the slippery customer whom I could catch only by engaging in this plan to make Rudolph king. Only for that would Herr Ottomkopf return to pay for his misdemeanor." He pointed a pudgy finger at Ottomkopf. "Do not deny it. The jewels smell even yet of cheese."

Ottomkopf's eyes were hollow. "You do this to me, Herr Dorp? You who were of my own regiment thirty years ago. You betray me now—"

Dorp struck his chest. "A Rudamian never forgets!" His little eyes narrowed. "A fine career I might have had in the Rudamian army. Already a young man, I was a lieutenant. What did you do?"

Ottomkopf groaned.

"For a paltry one hundred and fifty rudls—which I won honestly from you in playing poker—for a miserable one hundred and fifty rudls which you did not wish to pay me, you had me cashiered. In disgrace I come to America. But I vow, 'Some day he will pay the one hundred and fifty rudls. Through the nose!' " He pointed. "Take him, Joe, Jorge. I, Professor Dorp, have captured for you a criminal."

Lefty sighed. "Well, we've bagged a smuggler and a murderer—"

"Self-defense," repeated Rudolph.

"—and an O. P. A. violator."

Ferenz groaned into his hands.

"Think we can call it a day?"

"One moment, if you please." Hans bowed. "Before you leave for the police station, Your Highness, you will please to pay me for the sauerbraten you ate and the beer you drank." He drew himself high and thundered, "And which you sneaked out without paying for while I was answering the telephone."

"Pay him, Ferenz." Rudolph waved a languid hand.

Ferenz raised his head from his hands. "Pay him yourself," he said crossly. "For you," his lip drooped, "I will have to starve myself. The Board of Rations does not understand my needs." His voice zoomed, "Pay him yourself with my sixty-five thousand dollars."

"You didn't give me sixty-five thousand dollars," Rudolph retorted. "It was only seven thousand."

"Dorp!" Ferenz bellowed.

Dorp said, "It wasn't sixty-five thousand, Mr. Lessering. It was only ten thousand. Don't you remember that? Three thousand of it Herr Ottomkopf and I needed for expenses. Rudolph's bills in Mexico. The escape. Seven thousand we have given to Rudoph."

"It was sixty-five thousand," Ferenz insisted. "First twenty-five thousand. Then twenty-five more. And another fifteen. Add it up. Sixty-five thousand I turned over to Ruprecht to finance this flight—" He broke off. Silence was utter. His voice bubbled through. "Where is Ruprecht?" His voice filled the house. *"Where is Ruprecht?"*

Trudy's smile was apologetic. "I think by now he's on his way to Mexico."

"Mexico!" Ferenz faltered.

"I'm sorry. I didn't know until tonight, Furry, or I wouldn't have let him. He's wanted Rudolph's Mexican place for a long time. To make sort of a rich man's dude ranch out of it. That's why he thought up the idea of getting you to make Rudolph king. It was the only way he could borrow enough money from you—it's only a loan, really—and oust Rudolph at the same time. You'll get your money all paid back. He's going to make pots of it." Her voice was smaller. "And even if he doesn't it's only three years till he's thirty and he'll have Uncle Isaiah's estate. You don't have to worry one bit, Ferenz. He'll pay you back."

"Oh God," Ferenz groaned.

Johnnie'd had a funny feeling for some time that Rupe wasn't coming back with that champagne. He'd been right. He only hoped the bottles were left behind. He was pretty sure they weren't.

The law was forming ranks now. Johnnie said, "Before we go I'd like to ask Herr Dorp one thing. Why was he talking German on the subway?"

"I don't talk German," Dorp said. "That was Rudamian."

2.

Broadway looked about the same as it had twenty-four hours ago. Saturday night didn't seem to make much difference to New Yorkers. Every night was Saturday here. He, Johnnie, didn't think he'd care much about that kind of a town. You wouldn't know when it was time to celebrate.

He stood on the steps outside the front door of the Astor, right where Bill and Hank had told him to meet them. They ought to be turning up pretty soon now.

He hadn't had a lick of sleep but he didn't feel very tired. He'd seen New York and how. From the Battery to the Bronx. He hadn't missed a trick. Including the inside of Centre Street. He'd sure have a letter to write home to the folks this week. Take him a week to write it. They'd get a big kick out of all the sights he'd seen today. He'd been lucky that Trudy wasn't tied up. It was more fun sightseeing with a cute little blonde babe under your arm. Lucky too, that she'd wanted to make up to him for missing everything last night. She knew the town. Without her he'd never have thought of half the places to go.

He did feel kind of funny having her pay everything. But it was Ruprecht's party, she said. Ruprecht had given Trudy the folding dough to show Johnnie everything, including the best food he'd ever put down. Without Johnnie helping out last night, Ruprecht might not have got away in time. He might have been in the soup with the rest of them. Not that Rupe had done anything wrong. He'd simply made a suggestion and Ferenz had taken care of the rest. Ferenz would get his money back.

There was only one big disappointment left in Johnnie. None of them turned out to be Nazis. He would have liked to have captured a band of Nazis. Well, he'd have to take care of that when he got overseas. If they'd only hurry and ship him before the big push was over.

He looked up and down the street. No sign of Hank and Bill. He hoped they hadn't forgotten him. Then he turned his nose up to the sky. Stars up there. Not great big shiny ones like in Texas but stars just the same. Somewhere up above there was a plane. Trudy would be on her way to Mexico by now. She wasn't letting Rupe escape her. The first thing she was going to do there was send a bottle of champagne to Johnnie.

Couple of soldiers crossing Broadway now that might be Bill and Hank. They were Bill and Hank. Johnnie hunched back his shoulders. They'd be difficult at first but he could out-talk them. He had before. He came down the steps to meet them.

"Hi ya, fellows," he greeted.

They were relieved to see him. After that they were mad.

"Well," said Bill. "The missing link, I presume?"

"When did you think you were supposed to meet us?" Hank demanded. "Any night at nine? You think the Army gave us a pass to hang out in front of the Astor for the duration?"

"Cut the two-bit flap," Johnnie advised happily. "I'm here, ain't I?"

Bill's chin went up. "So you got lost again, did you?"

"I did not," Johnnie denied hotly. "I knew where I was all the time."

"Where were you?" Hank wanted to know. "Where have you been?"

Johnnie took a deep breath. "I've been everywhere. To the Bronx zoo and the Aquarium and Grant's

Tomb, that isn't much; and a conducted tour of Radio City and rowing on the lake in Central Park; and Park Avenue, that's nothing but apartments, and Harlem—" He stopped for another breath.

"Alone?" Bill's face was unbelieving.

It would be nice to say, "Yes, alone," and get Bill over the idea that he, Johnnie, was a hick. But that wouldn't be fair to Trudy. He shook his head. "No, not alone."

"Who went with you?"

"A girl."

Bill and Hank gave him the wolf gleam. "Where is she?"

He said happily, "She left for Mexico. So sorry, chums."

It was all going well. But disappointment couldn't silence these lugs long enough. Bill was too smart. Bill asked carefully now, "Where were you last night?"

Johnnie said with vagueness, "I went for a ride on the subway." He wouldn't ever tell them about last night. They would never trust him out of their sight again. They would think he was crazy. They wouldn't understand it had all been strictly accidental.

"In the subway," said Bill. "And then?"

Johnnie talked fast. "I had some champagne, real champagne." He'd better get these guys started before they got too nosey. The money he hadn't touched was burning a hole in his sock. "I'll tell you what, let's go buy a bottle of champagne right now. My treat." He grabbed an arm on either side of him. "And then let's go to the Stage Door Canteen. Maybe we'll see Sonja Henie."

He didn't want to waste tonight too. When a guy had a weekend pass, he expected a little fun.